Issue No. 2

Matter

Guest Authors: Michel Faber
Janice Galloway
E.A. Markham
& Ali Smith

MATTER ISSUE NO.2 • Joint Editors: Leigh Money & Emily Pedder • Design: Johnie Clayton • Contributing Editors: Carolyn Waudby & Laura K. Watson • Advertising & Fundraising: Bryony Doran • Press & Publicity: Emily Brett • Contents: © The Individual Authors 2002 • With special thanks to: Sarah Broughton • Elaine Bull • Jason Starmer • Dr. Steven Earnshaw & Sheffield Hallam University • Published by: Ink, London • Printed by Biddles Ltd, Woodbridge Park, Guildford •

ISBN 0-9543150-0-6
www.mattermagazine.co.uk
Contact: mattermagazine@yahoo.co.uk

Contents

The Shadow Gulls [an extract]
Jason Starmer

Once lunch was over my parents took Lee and I to swim in the sea. We wandered west along the shore as the waves rushed the sand to swirl at our calves; following the curve of the bay till we reached the rock outcrop marking the end of the beach. It was here that the lagoon drained into the ocean, running alongside the rocky ledges in a shallow gully about a foot deep.

My father climbed onto the rocks to look out at the horizon while my mother settled herself on the sand. Lee and

I played in the wash, rolling with the brackish water down toward the surge of the waves.

And it was here, a place we'd played in so often before, a place favoured by many parents as the safest on the beach, that Lee drowned.

It had all seemed so simple. Even as it started it seemed nothing more than an inconvenience.

Lee following me in the soft push of water from the lagoon, skimming over the sandy bed of the wash and into the salty foam of the waves. I, standing, turning, reaching behind me to empty a pocket of sand from the seat of my costume. And Lee, his face showing a look of surprise and confusion, still halfway up toward the lagoon, the water pressing him against the rock.

"Les," he called, "my leg is stuck."

Lee had jammed his leg into a space created by the current below one of the shelves of rock. Had the sand around him been a little more built up there would have been no space at all. A little less sand and his leg would have passed under the rock unhindered. But the sand's level rose and fell with each tide, with each wave. A question of inches really, a question of luck.

By the time I had waded back to him Lee was stuck up to his thigh, a few moments later, when my mother arrived, he was wedged in up to his waist.

"I don't understand," said my mother, trying to drag him out. "Does it hurt?"

"No, not really," replied Lee, calmly.

"Les, go fetch your father," said my mother. And then, as I walked away, "I don't understand," for the second time. She would repeat that phrase throughout the day and for much of the next few months.

.

When I found my father and brought him back to the wash Lee was still in place. My mother had not let him slip any further under the rock nor had she managed to draw him out at all. With each minute the river must have pressed another handful of sand against him, until the grains around him were packed as solid as the rock above.

My father replaced my mother in the water behind Lee, his forearms hooked into Lee's armpits.

"This doesn't look that difficult," he said. "Lee, does it hurt you when I pull you like this."

"No."

"I mean, is it scratching you when I move you? Does the rock scratch your legs?"

"I'm not moving."

We must have sat that way for a full minute before my father sent my mother for the help.

"You'll be okay Lee. The lifeguards will get you out in no time. They'll know what to do," said my father once my mother ran off across the beach.

The following forty-five minutes passed calmly enough. A crowd had begun to gather at the end of the beach, a loose knot of the curious and concerned, held in the orbit of Lee and my father. People came forward occasionally to make suggestions and the lifeguards organised a group of men who tried to dig my brother free. But, after fifteen minutes of noisy splashing they had made no discernable headway, the water replacing the muddy sand that they scooped away almost immediately. Lee, rather than lying parallel to the flow of the gully, was angled away from us, his legs far further under the ledge of rock than the men could reach, digging as they were under a foot of rushing water. It was eventually decided that sandbags were needed in order to stem the flow from the lagoon and allow Lee to be excavated like some fragile archaeological relic. A lifeguard told us that the fire brigade had been called and all we could do was wait. After this the men stopped digging and retreated to the dry sand on the beach, returning to their own families, their own children.

In all this our family remained impassive. Lee with the solemn eyes of a stoic, my father holding my brother's head to his chest and my mother and I, on the rocks above, looking down in patient silence.

The arrival of the fire brigade coincided with the final ebbing of the tide and, as the firemen organised a human-chain to pass sandbags the length of the beach, so began the steady advance of the sea. Once all of the sandbags had been passed man to man and the firemen began to arrange them across the mouth of the lagoon the waves had reached the level they had been when Lee first became stuck, rushing up to swirl at his belly and occasionally foaming at his chin. When, eventually, the flow from the lagoon had been entirely contained the waves were rushing into his face every few minutes and people around us began to agree that the rising tide posed a threat which had been entirely overlooked.

"It's the spring tide, you see," I overheard a lifeguard

telling my mother. "If it had been neaps it would be different."

Once it had been decided that the sandbags were worthless we were informed that the fire brigade had decided that an enclosure needed to be erected around Lee and my father, some type of fence to hold the water at bay. My father was passed a snorkel, which he fitted into my brother's mouth, twisting the mouthpiece so that the end of the tube was higher than the level of the larger waves. Each time the water rushed toward him my father would pinch Lee's nose closed and, bowing his head forward, remind him to keep his lips tight around the tube. When the wave retreated he'd wipe the water from Lee's face as he re-emerged, blinking, into the air.

But the materials needed for Lee's rescue were not easily located and soon, as the afternoon faded and the sea began to darken and silver, his face was more often under the water than above it. Occasionally the waves would rise above the level of the snorkel and my father would block it with his hand. Lee, too tired by now, would swallow water and then cough it up so that it bubbled out of the tube and hazed the air before my father's face with a mist of breath and spit.

"He's getting water in his mouth," said my father.

"Blow in the tube," said a lifeguard.

"No, don't blow. Suck," said someone else.

My brother's fingers, gripping my father's forearm, clenched tighter, the skin around the nails puckered and white.

"There's a breathing-tank in the truck." said a fireman, "Do you think he'll be able to use it? I mean, I'm sure this won't take much longer… but just in case?"

"Yes," said my father, "I think we'd better."

.

I can pinpoint now the exact moment of Lee's death. I think that both my mother and myself, watching from above, knew the change for what it was. My father, and the people busy around him, noticed my mother's cries first and what they implied only after.

The fireman with the tank was running back across the beach, his stride uneven, the cylinder banging, with each step, against his right knee. In my memory I see my father's face below us, looking up questioningly at my mother, "Where is he? Where's the tank?" he says.

"He's coming," she says. "He's almost here."

My father looks down at the end of the snorkel, drops of water rattling at its mouth as Lee fights to breath out.

Another wave rushes his chest, spilling into the dark hollow of the tube and then receding and there, darting and fluttering in the water, is Lee's hand, trailing in the current, no longer fastened to my father's arm. That hand, suddenly adrift, its whiteness flickering below the surface, turning and shining like a fish, is abruptly the focus of my attention. I hear my mother's voice, high and rising further in pitch, without words, a steady climb of breaking notes. My father looks up at us and then down, his eyes following ours to watch the hand break the surface, roll once and subside again, tumbling in the flow with the freedom of the inanimate.

"Jesus," he says, "Oh Jesus," and arches forward into the water, pressing his body to Lee's beneath a filigree of foam.

•

I wasn't there when they finally brought my brother's body out. I had been sent home, back to my sisters who had been phoned to prepare them for my arrival and for the news I would bring. Not long after Lee's hand had lost its hold on my father's wrist and Lee himself had floated free of our lives my mother rose from the water to take charge of the practicalities of her loss. She spoke to a lifeguard and asked him if he would mind driving me home, she even remembered to ask how long he had had his license.

"Tell your sisters we won't be long," she said, crouching before me.

I nodded and watched over her shoulder as the firemen erected a semi-circular structure of corrugated plastic around my father and brother. When they started to pump the water out my mother gently steered me away before climbing down the rocks to kneel in the water alongside my father.

I would later be told how the fireman lit the area of their work once I had left, how, after pumping the water away they dug a trench, first alongside my brother, and then extended it under him until they could ease him free.

I picture the scene the moment he begins to slip from under the rock – the artificial brightness of the emergency lights; the orient shimmer of the water, dark and high, beyond the wet plastic; the harshly lit blonde of Lee's head against the densely slicked curling of my father's chest; the dusting of freckles and peeling skin at his sunburnt shoulders. And my brother's hand, that dreadful tumbling hand, held still and solid between my mother's palms.

My mother would later say that it was then that she realized that Lee was truly gone. She would describe the heaviness of his limbs, the limp weight of him as my father shuffled forward on his knees trying, even then, to keep Lee's face above what little water was left around them.

But for me Lee's real leaving came not at the beach but as I lay in bed later that night. It was the last time in my life that I would experience what it was to be a twin, to know how it felt in another's skin. My body seemed to rock and settle in the sheets, the memory of the ocean-swell a ghost of movement deep in my joints, and, as my eyes began to falter, I knew what it was like for Lee… I was, for one last time, my brother – feeling the soft rush and pull of the sea as, through a shimmer of water, my world closed to dark.

The Fireyard

Peter Daniels Luczinski

At the back, the last room, lucky to get it.
The whole hotel smells of damp curry,
facilities not special.

I settle down with the old t.v. showing Winter Olympics,
two rival skaters perform their separate circles
but I shift across to the local Chinese stations.
Men in suits all the same shade of grey,
seems to be the Taiwanese Parliament.

The spyhole lens in the door
is fitted the wrong way round
– hm? There's a label in my new
underpants – "Inspected by Carol" –
I stick it over.

Through the venetian blinds, outside
I spy the Fire Station yard, the men
idly shooting hoops, playing a hose on a car.
How many visitors must bless this
pent-up exercise. San Francisco
in its own bored heat, ready for flames.

Tiger in the Jardin Zoologique

Carolyn Waudby

Stretched out on a weary side his amber hide
gleams; black ribs, a tribal gown,
heave in the Paris sun.

We think he sleeps but one ear
turns like a dish, hoping to catch
the tropical stir of a leaf.
One paw extends, testing the sinews of his leg.

"Il est fatigue. Il fait dos-dos," the children are told.
Then, the black-hooped tail flails the air,
strikes ground, stops breath.
He is the ringmaster;
Every slight of muscle demands respect.

It is nothing to him.
Minute on minute again we wait.
He raises a head, cuffed with white,
stares unmoved into distant skies,

And yawns, to remind us he could crush a man –
pierce a heart with teeth like daggers
worn around our necks.

Too many fruits.

Some of those exotic ones like mango and papaya and guava...

There's just too many.

Mmm?

Yeah, no, totally.

Too many fruits.

[two men at a train station]

VANILLA-
BRIGHT
LIKE
EMINƎM

Michel Faber

Don, son of people no longer living, husband of Alice, father of Drew and Aleesha, is very, very close to experiencing the happiest moment of his life.

It's 10.03 according to his watch, and he is travelling to Inverness, tired and ever-so-slightly anxious in case he falls asleep between now and when the train reaches the station, and misses his cue to say to Alice, Drew and Aleesha: "OK, this is Inverness, let's move it." His wife and children are dozing, worn out by sightseeing; the responsibility rests on his shoulders. He doesn't know that the train terminates in Inverness and that everyone will be told by loudspeakers to get out; he imagines it rolling smoothly on, ferrying them farther south, stealthily leaving their pre-booked bed & breakfast behind. This is his first visit to Scotland; the film in his camera has only two shots left; there's no Diet Coke on the refreshment trolley; his wife's head sags forward, giving her a double chin; big raindrops skid silently against the thick glass of the train windows.

Don and his family have occupied the table seating on both sides of the central aisle: eight seats in all, for four people. He reassures himself that this is OK: the train isn't very full. Plus, he and his family are big people: Americans, head-and-shoulders above most of the other passengers. Drew, just turned fifteen, is five-eleven; Don is six-two.

Both of them have hands like boxers. Three hours ago, on the way down to breakfast in an overheated hotel near Dunrobin Castle, Drew had a little blow-out and said "Fuck you, Dad", but they've made up since then, and Don is two minutes away from the big moment.

Alice and Aleesha are across the aisle, slumped opposite each other, their sports bags propped in the window seats, too bulky for the overhead baggage rack. Aleesha, still a child at thirteen despite her budding breasts and chapped white nail polish, has snoozed off in the middle of reading Buffy The Vampire Slayer. Her thin arm dangles in the aisle, bracelets of chewed multi-coloured cotton hooped around her knobbly wrist. Her mother is dreaming uneasily, digging her head into the back of the seat as if registering her frustration with its pitiless design. Alice is forty, and hates being forty. Every month, three days before her period, she starts complaining about her body and its worsening hear, which takes some guessing.

The happiest moment of his life so far, besides the one he's about to experience, was when he saw Alice waiting for him outside what was then still called Kentucky Fried Chicken, and she smiled at him, and they both knew they were going to drive straight to Ben and Lisa's empty beach house and make love to each other for the first time. Those three days at Ben and Lisa's place were magnificent, and he felt such joy in bed with Alice, getting to know her in that way, but her smile when he approached her – that smile of welcome and anticipation and conviction that she was doing the right thing – that was a more memorable thrill than anything they did afterwards. Standing in that doorway under an icon of Colonel Sanders, she was wearing a little black dress with a tan raincoat loosely buckled over it: very French, or so he thought then, never having been to France but having seen movies set there.

Today Alice is wearing a khaki-coloured T-shirt and a loose flannel shirt over that: travelling gear. They were in France in '97, arguing with the kids about the Louvre versus Eurodisney.

Don looks down under the table. He's wearing trainers on his huge feet, military pants. In Scotland, 'pants' means underwear. His military pants have lots of pockets and zips and drawstrings and toggles, more than anyone could find a use for. It's a fashion thing, and he wonders if he's too old for it. Yesterday, Aleesha was sitting next to him on a different train from this one, and she unzipped a pocket in the calf of his pants, just to see what was in it. It was a toddlerish action, an innocent gesture of playfulness and boredom, but he felt the charge of her maturing sexuality and was disturbed by it. "That's kinda dumb, Dad," she'd said, dabbling her fingers in the unzipped slit of fabric, a pocket too narrow for anything bigger than a pen, assuming you'd want a pen stowed against your calf. Idly, Aleesha had zipped him up again.

He looks across the table at his son. An inflatable neck-cushion is acting as a pillow for Drew's cheek; his brow rests on his muscular forearms; his hands are loosely balled into fists. From this angle, he's not the world's most good-looking kid. His nose is in the process of mushrooming into the same bulbous schnozzle that all the males in Don's family have had for generations; his lips are swollen, bee-stung, more feminine than Aleesha's – an observation that would enrage him if he knew. And, all over his skull, where there used to be a shaggy brown mop of Heavy Metal hair, is now… The Haircut. The haircut they argued over endlessly.

"You can't bleach your hair like Eminem. You'll look like an idiot. He looks like an idiot."

Drew had sighed, his shoulders hunched against the weight of the pre-senile ignorance being heaped on them.

"Eminem is cool. Besides, it's my hair, and my money."

Frightening, how a sentence of only ten words could provide fuel for so many hours of fierce dispute over a period of days. Whose money was Drew's money? What did he have to do to make it his own? Was it his if he chose to spend it on boy scout crap or some old Bruce Springsteen record, but not if he spent it on Eminem? And whose hair was Drew's hair, exactly? (Don felt like a maniac arguing about this, but on the other hand wasn't it true that he and Alice had created that hair, and the head on which it grew, one night – or maybe one day – fifteen years ago? Every follicle on Drew's scalp was made according to their secret genetic recipe, and nurtured from egg to brunette boy.) Who did Drew think he was fooling, pledging fellowship with ghetto youth and the hip-hop scene, chanting along with lyrics about smacking bitches and fuckin' wid de wrong niggaz, when he was a white kid living with his folks in the suburbs of West Springfield, with a holiday in Scotland on the horizon? To which Drew's response was that maybe he wouldn't be living with his folks much longer, not the way their attitude was making him puke, and they could shove their trip to Scotland, he'd rather hang out with his friends here, and anyway, Eminem was white, so what's your problem? Which provoked Don to tell his son exactly what his problem was. Eminem, he said, was a walking invitation for kids to give up on everything and wallow in negativity. Thanks to rap stars like him, kids were being sold pessimism the way they were once sold chewing gum. Kids who were too young to know a damn thing about the big wide world were coming to the conclusion that Planet Earth was rotten to the core and there was nothing to be done about it except buy CDs and T-shirts.

Alice, trying to stop the conflict getting too global, suggested that Eminem had the right shape of face for bleached, close-cropped hair, but that it wouldn't suit Drew's features at all.

"It's only fuckin' hair!" Drew had yelled. "What is it

with you people?" He was cursing a lot lately, whenever he got mad, mostly at his father, but even sometimes at his mother. Every time he yelled Fuck, Aleesha would flinch, as if someone had just thrown a glass against the wall.

Now, Drew lies sleeping on his inflatable cushion, his arms freshly sunburnt, his hair close-cropped and creamy-white. His shoulders are well-muscled, almost a man's shoulders, and Don realises all of a sudden that his son is better-built than Eminem can ever be – taller, stronger, fitter, handsomer. Aleesha wakes from her doze, looks at the window in case it's Inverness already, then looks to her father for confirmation that it's not. He shakes his head and she smiles. Why the smile? He doesn't know, but he smiles back. Aleesha leans sideways into the aisle, stretching her arm across the empty space towards her brother. In her hand is the comb she was using as a bookmark just before she fell asleep. Carefully, oh-so-slowly, she runs the teeth of her comb through her brother's hair. Time slows right down. The comb lifts the nap of Drew's crop, revealing rich brown roots under the bleached exterior. The way it lifts and resettles as the comb passes through it is mesmerising, like watching wheat being rustled by the breeze.

Drew doesn't stir; he's either deeply asleep or determined to ignore his sister. She combs on, tenderly, aware of her dad watching her, aware of the spell she's casting over him. Drew's hair lifts and re-settles, lifts and re-settles, the bristles soft as a brand-new paintbrush, luxury bristle, mink fur. It's a good

haircut after all, damn it. In fact, it's the best haircut Drew
has ever had, the best haircut on this train, the best haircut
in all of Scotland north of Inverness, maybe the best haircut
in the world.

Out of the corner of his eye, Don sees Alice repositioning
herself, laying her head down on her bag, shifting her weight
from her butt to her side. The swell of her butt is sexy, and
he gets a glimpse of her naked flesh where the T-shirt has
come untucked from her jeans. He still wants her. He's looking
forward to the next time they're alone together in a bed, at
home or not at home, anywhere where he can run his palms
over her warm skin and stroke her hair off her face.

His son snoozes on the table in front of him, a big man
of a son, hair feathery and vanilla-bright, almost too bright
in the sunlight, and above it hovers the beautiful hand and
arm of his daughter, coloured cotton bracelets dangling from
her wrist, which flexes rhythmically as she grooms the white
pelt of her one and only brother, grooms him pointlessly, for
he's as combed as combed can be, except that there is a point,
because this is the happiest moment of Don's life.

In thirty seconds from now, a refreshments trolley will
come down the aisle, and Aleesha will be asked by a stunted
guy in a uniform to move her arm please, and she'll put it
back and Don's happiness will ebb a little, just enough to
make it no longer the happiest moment of his life, but that's
OK, because it was a long moment, longer than Alice's smile

in the doorway of what has since been renamed KFC. In fifty seconds from now, Aleesha will ask her mother if she can have a chocolate bar, and Drew, still slumped motionless on the table, will say, in a deep voice and distinctly, "Is there any Pepsi?" In half an hour, they will be in Inverness; in three days they will be home; in two years, Aleesha will announce to her parents that she's always hated the name Aleesha, it sounds like one of those dumb-ass names that black people invent, and she's going to call herself Ellen from now on. And in five years, despite her parents' confident predictions, Ellen won't have grown out of being Ellen, she'll still be Ellen and she'll have had an abortion and her smile will be different, lopsided and a little discoloured by smoking, but she'll be engaged to a man who adores her, and pregnant with a baby she intends to keep.

And by then, Drew will be living in South America somewhere, and Don and Alice will never see him anymore, and their friends will say that they must be very proud of what he's trying to achieve there, and they'll say yes, they're proud, and they'll show these people a photograph of Drew on a construction site in what looks like a shanty town, and he'll be wearing glasses perched on his gigantic schnozzle, his dark brown hair slicked with water and sweat. And Alice will go and make coffee, walking stiffly because of her tennis shoulder which isn't tennis shoulder at all but the first signs of the illness that will kill her when she's fifty-nine, and after that Don will tell everyone he'll never be able to love another women, but three years later he'll marry one of the people he said this to, and she'll be warm and funny and a great cook and not as good in bed as Alice but he'll never tell her that, he'll die before he tells her that, because she'll make him happy, happier than he ever expected to be in his old age, happier than any of the other miserable old coots that live in his neighbourhood, happier than he's ever been in fact, except for maybe a couple of isolated moments, like the smile of a young woman waiting to be his lover, her face glowing in the light of a fast-food franchise, and like the hand of his daughter floating above the head of his son, on this morning in a Scottish train, the haircut making everything worthwhile, shining so bright it leaves a pattern on your retina when you close your eyes, vanilla-bright like Eminem.

The Cur

● *[an extract]*

tain

Niyati Keni

Mahesh, a waiter and ambitious but untalented poet, has returned home after eight years to reclaim a lost love – his cousin, Rita. For eight years, he has led his family to believe he owns his own restaurant. His and Rita's parents share a flat which they have divided into territories with a central curtain through which they do not communicate except to snipe indirectly. Mahesh has been living in London where he is involved with an English woman who Vanita, his mother, has spoken to on the phone and assumed to be his cleaner. Wanting him to settle down, his parents have arranged an introduction to a suitable girl for the night of his return.

ACT TWO, SCENE ONE

The Bombay flat. The two rear sections are living areas separated by the central curtain. Each contains a settee with printed Indian cotton throws, the right also contains a fat wicker armchair, in which sits Mahesh's father, Ram. Both have small wall tables with telephones and dining tables with chairs. The left has an old mahogany bureau against one wall. The right a wooden dresser. A Persian rug covers the floor of both sides, passing under the curtain – it has plainly been there from the beginning. At the front, also bisected by a trellis, is the gallery which has a wooden railing and potted plants on both sides. It looks out over the street. There are thin wicker chairs of various styles and a hanging hurricane lamp on both sides of it. The colours and lights are earthy, reddish, lived in, worn. Only the rear right section is currently lit. Mahesh enters this section with a large shoulder bag. He dumps it on the floor. His mother greets him. His father raises a glass from where he sits.

> VANITA
> You must be exhausted, Mahesh. Come and
> sit down. Tip your father off that chair and
> make yourself comfortable.

> RAM
> What'll you have to drink, son?

> VANITA
> A nice cup of tea no doubt.

MAHESH
Do you have any gin?

VANITA
(surprised)
Gin?

RAM
That's my boy. I have no tonic, though. Only
soda. But we can get some in a jiffy. What
would you prefer?

MAHESH
Tonic would be great. But soda will do. Don't
rush out just for me.

VANITA
Your father doesn't rush, darling.

Ram strolls out to gallery and leans over railing, whistles loudly,
then yells.

RAM
Hey, Bhai. Get Ashok to send up some tonic
will you? And some limes. And some ice.

VANITA
Hasn't been within six thousand miles of you
in seven years and your DNA still manages to
ruin the boy.

RAM
Let him relax. He's only just arrived.

Ram starts pouring Mahesh a drink.

VANITA
We can eat whenever you're ready, Mahesh.
Although, if we wait till eight o'clock, Lalita
and her daughter will be here. You might
remember little Anju, perhaps?

MAHESH
(disinterestedly)
No.

VANITA
She was in Rita's class at school. Attractive
girl. Almost finished her accountancy exams.
She'd make a good wife for a businessman.

MAHESH
How are you both?

VANITA
Fine, fine. We're dying to hear all about your
restaurant. If you wait till Lalita and Anju
arrive you can tell us all together.

Mahesh accepts glass from father.

MAHESH
I see the curtain is still up.

RAM
That bloody thing will be up till the last one
of us dies no doubt. And then it'll be recycled
as a shroud. We're nothing if not
environmentally conscious.

VANITA
Must you be so morbid? It's the last thing he
needs after traveling so far. We've missed you
so much, Mahesh. You've lost weight. All that
puppy fat's fallen away. My little boy's grown up.

RAM
The nature of things. Children grow up.
Parents grow sideways.

VANITA
Speak for yourself.

MAHESH
(firm)
I eat properly. I exercise. The business is fine.
Everything's fine.

VANITA
So sensible to employ a cleaner. How would
you find time to keep things tidy while
running a business? I hope she's thorough.
What does she look like?

MAHESH
She's old. Very old. Why?

VANITA
You can tell a lot about a person's attitude to
work from how they look. The young these
days take no pride in hard work. They act as
if the world owes them a living. I blame MTV.
MTV and too much sex. Sex everywhere.
Advertising cars, movies, food. You can't
separate it from day to day life.

RAM
Of course you can't separate it from day to day
life. It's a basic biological fact. It's no wonder
people are obsessed by it.

VANITA
I'm not obsessed by it.

RAM
No.

MAHESH
(hastily)
How was the funeral?

RAM
Frosty.

MAHESH
Are they still planning to hold the 12th day feast?

VANITA
It's in two days time. It's good that you're here for it. We'll go and show our faces. I won't have people saying that we can't even be civil to our own family at a time of crisis.

MAHESH
What's happening about the wedding?

VANITA
Nothing definite yet.

RAM
Has the business starting paying its own way yet, son? Cleared all the business loans and what have you? In the black at last?

VANITA
Don't interrogate him, Ram. He's come for
a holiday too. So, Mahesh, are you seeing
anyone?

RAM
Own car? Own teeth?

MAHESH
Seeing?

VANITA
You know. Romantically. You always were
such an innocent. Head in the clouds or in
a book.

MAHESH
No, I'm not seeing anyone.

VANITA
I see. Good, good. It's almost eight. I'll start
warming things up. Mahesh, will you help
your father arrange the table? Don't forget to
wash your hands.

RAM
He's not a child anymore.

VANITA
You too. With soap.

A cheerful Bollywood film music accompanies the following actions, fading out before Ram speaks again. Ram, Mahesh and Vanita get up and leave. A soft light grows on the left side. Rita's mother, Mira, comes in from the kitchen and sits down in a chair. She flips open a magazine and quietly starts reading. A moment later, Rita walks in through the front door. She slings her bag onto the settee and leans down to kiss her mother. She goes offstage into the kitchen. On the right, the doorbell rings. Ram re-enters to answer. A man enters with bottles of tonic, limes and a bowl of ice on a tray and puts them on the table. Ram pulls out some money, pays him. The man namastes, goes. Mahesh enters wiping his hands on a towel. Rita returns on the left with a tray bearing a pitcher and two glasses. She sits down with a newspaper.

RAM
Another drop of jet fuel, son?

Ram pours a generous G&T.

MAHESH
Yes please. You know, Papa, nothing's changed at all here. It's like I'm a young boy again with all my dreams ahead of me and all my doubts around me.

At the sound of Mahesh's voice, Rita looks up.

>   RAM
>   (thoughtful)
>   Promise me you'll never let drinking replace
>   dreaming.

Ram holds out Mahesh's drink.

>   MAHESH
>   (startled)
>   I promise

Mahesh takes the glass.

>   VANITA
>   (from offstage)
>   Hurry up troops. They'll be here any minute.

Mahesh and Ram arrange the table – plates, glasses etc from the
dresser. The doorbell rings.

>   VANITA
>   Mahesh, will you get the door please, darling?

Mahesh goes to the door. Lalita, a stout, middle aged Indian woman
and her rather thin daughter, Anju, enter.

RAM
Lalita. Anju. Can I get you both a drink? Tea?
Or something stronger?

LALITA
I'll join you for a scotch and soda, Ram. Anju
will have some tea. Or fruit juice if you have any.
Mahesh, haven't you grown? You remember
my daughter Anju?

Rita puts down her paper. Mira looks at her, then at the curtain.
Rita looks down guiltily. Ram starts pouring a scotch.

MAHESH
(curt)
No. Should I?

LALITA
(a little shocked)
She was in Rita's year at school. She
remembers you.

MAHESH
(to Anju)
Do you speak?

ANJU
(*indignant*)
Of course I speak.

MAHESH
It's as well in here. It seems imprudent to let
people speak for you.

RAM
Was that juice or tea, Anju?

ANJU
(*looking at the salver on the table*)
I see you have fresh lime and ice. I'll have a
gin and tonic please.

LALITA
Anju!

ANJU
I'm twenty four, mother. It's not like I've
never tasted alcohol.

LALITA
Make it a small one then please, Ram.

RAM
Your scotch or Anju's G&T?

LALITA
(hesitating, guiltily)
Both.

RAM
(pouring clumsily)
Oops. By some quirk of quantum physics,
small doesn't seem to be possible in this flat.
You can always leave it if you don't want it.

ANJU
That'll be fine, thankyou, Uncle Ram.

Vanita re-enters with a plate of snacks. Ram settles back into a
chair and sips his drink.

MAHESH
If he was your uncle, that would make me
your cousin. And then all this matchmaking
would be immoral. Isn't that right, Papa?

On the left, Rita is startled, looks guiltily at her mother, goes
back to her paper. Mira puts her magazine down for a minute
and stares across at the curtain then at her daughter. She continues
to eavesdrop.

RAM
(*vaguely*)
Yes, yes.

LALITA
You misunderstand. It's just a casual visit.

ANJU
I think you mean illegal. Except in Jammu
and Kashmir where marriage between first
cousins is acceptable. What's your point?

MAHESH
(*hesitating*)
No point. It was just an observation.

VANITA
(*uneasily*)
Don't be offended by Mahesh. He's just a little
jet lagged.

ANJU
Jet lag makes you tired, not insane.

VANITA
He has some of Ram's blood in him too. He's
bound to be a little mad.

On the left, Mira starts reading again.

>MAHESH
>Is that the blood or the alcohol that makes
>him mad? Or the death of dreams?

Mira snickers.

>LALITA
>You haven't been away so long that you've
>forgotten it's just our way. All young people call
>their elders 'aunt' and 'uncle'. It reminds us
>we're just one large family. In a spiritual sense.

>MAHESH
>It keeps us children and you adults. However
>old we get.

>ANJU
>What would be your alternative?

>MAHESH
>Everybody has a name, don't they?

>LALITA
>It seems rather disrespectful to call elders by
>their first name and rather formal to call
>them by their titles or surnames when they've
>known you since you were in nappies.

MAHESH
It seems rather fruitless to be mired in
tradition when you've outgrown it.

Mira grows increasingly interested.

LALITA
Only outcasts outgrow tradition. Civilised
people stay within it.

MAHESH
Surely the more developed one gets, the less
one needs tradition. It's only there to preserve
the power structure as it is.

LALITA
Such arrogance. You always were rather
spoilt.

Mira laughs out loud.

VANITA
Lalita!

LALITA
Well, he was.

MIRA
No doubt, still is.

MAHESH
At least when I reach your age, I won't have
spent my entire life stuck in the same damn
rut.

VANITA
Mahesh!

ANJU
No. I'm sure you'll have exchanged it for
another one.

Mahesh glares at Anju but says nothing.

VANITA
(*placatory*)
Mahesh, I'm sure you're tired, but, Lalita and
Anju have come just to see you.

MAHESH
Why?

VANITA
(*defensive*)
Why not? They were just asking after you. I
thought it might be nice. No particular
reason.

MAHESH
(to Anju)
You're single. That's why you're here. This is
an introduction and I'm supposed to charm
you.

RAM
He's quick on the draw, my son.

ANJU
(to Mahesh)
I imagine you must find that rather difficult.

LALITA
You run your own restaurant, I hear. No
doubt you're used to being brusque with your
staff.

ANJU
Some people would say that kindness and
courtesy are more effective in people
management.

MAHESH
God, how nauseating.

RAM
(quickly)

It's probably the ice. You're used to London
water now. I'll pour you another without.
Lalita, Anju, shall I top you up as well?

ANJU
I think this much alcohol will have killed any
bacteria by now. I'm fine, Uncle Ram.

RAM
Now you know why I'm as healthy as a horse.
My brother-in-law, hardly drank at all. And
now he's dead and I'm still blundering
through life. Rather a perverse little twist of
fate, don't you think?

Mira gasps. There is an awkward silence. Vanita rises rather
desperately.

VANITA
I think I'll bring the food through. Lalita,
would you give me a hand?

LALITA
I hope you've not made too much. I don't
think we'll be staying for long.

They exit to the kitchen.

RAM
So, Anju, how is the accountancy world?

ANJU
As energetic as usual, Uncle Ram. Actually,
I've been thinking about starting up my own
business. Perhaps Mahesh would give me
some tips. Did you start your business from
scratch?

MAHESH
Oh yes. In fact, I started as a waiter. Now I
own a restaurant that seats over a hundred
people. It has an indoor water garden.

ANJU
Probably the sound of trickling water is good
for digestion.

RAM
Though bad for the prostate.

MAHESH
(*ignoring both comments, prodding the curtain.*)
Real plants. Real water.

Mira is annoyed by the curtain being moved. She gets up to swat the
movement with her magazine, but restrains herself just short of it.

ANJU
The latter would seem sensible.

MAHESH
I thought about adding in a hydroelectric dam
but decided that might be a little ostentatious.

ANJU
(*coldly*)
Yes, I imagine it would appear brazen.

MAHESH
We get celebrities in there all the time.

ANJU
Anyone I'd know of?

MAHESH
I doubt it. Lots of Saudi royalty. The
occasional athlete.

ANJU
I picture you all jostling for head space. It
must get quite fraught.

Ram and Mira both giggle simultaneously. Then stop as they hear
each other.

MAHESH
(crossly)
It's easy to knock success.

RAM
(placatory)
It's easiest of all to give up and not even try
to succeed. You've amounted to more than
your old father already.

ANJU
You're a kind man, Uncle Ram. No-one who
knows you would dispute that.

MIRA
That much is true.

RAM
Would anyone like another?

MAHESH
Why not?

ANJU
No thanks – I haven't finished this one yet.

Lalita and Vanita return bearing platters of food which they place
on the table.

VANITA

Look, Lalita. They haven't killed each other
yet. That's an auspicious sign. Come on
everyone, let's eat. One can't argue on an
empty tank.

The Search

E.A. Markham

They saw him coming, of course, talked to him
in a language meant for grown-ups: structurally,
the house is sound, load-bearing walls intact:
a bit of damp, y'know, in the basement, underground
river, and all that; and the street, though tricky to say
like that Cambridge College, is something you'll soon
be using to advantage. The gentrification
has begun, the old dying or being moved out, couples
and restaurants taking their place. And, hey presto,
the search is done. Oh yes. Legally OK.

And on his private list of things to check
nothing is ticked off: how to read the statistics
of where it's safe to live? For in this street
in this town, if what they say is right,
someone is pretending to be something else;
and three, maybe four, ah, torturers of a domestic kind
smirk in their sitting-rooms; and who will point out
the house where a dirty word we needn't say squats
and soils our politics? Again, between here
and the High Street how is the resident murderer
without a scar on his face, to be identified?

When he invites a friend to toast this latest Safe House
she says well done, darling, and wonders
if he deserves it, for even though his hands
are clean she thinks perhaps he can live with
the neighbours from hell who won't invade his sleep
as they do hers. Anticipating her resentment
he tells a story from the poet Che Qianzi
of two people dreaming of an elephant,
and whether they dreamt the same elephant –
for an elephant is a large thing for one dreamer to encounter –
and she is reconciled to his stroke of luck

But what can he do to complete this search
and cleanse the street? The Agency, uninterested
in this level of hygiene, does not supply
new air, or a soap that launders memory.
So he must compromise, like staying in a bad marriage
for the sake of the children or the image.
Or because it's the same or worse elsewhere. (For outside
the house the world comes to us in a blitz of Headlines
and our friends fly away from the don't-call-them-massacres.)
So, dear god, pretend that life is short and you are old;
and settle for a scaled-down Truth and Reconciliation
Commission for your street. And like the parent
body, over there, don't ask for Reparations.

Yes, it worked those times when
we were maybe three and five
and always wanted to discover

the one hiding in the next room
or under the table, no embarrassment
at squeals of delight

on discovery. It was the best
game ever, even after the squealing
tightened into something else.

and the seekers were no longer
family. Times remembered
when I lay a trail so private

only you could find me:
how clever you were tracing
clues softer than thrown ribbon

or rose-petals, clues
sometimes soft as scent dissolving
into air. When you began to lose

your way I had to mark the ground
with harder evidence – things
branded valuable in themselves –

to my hiding-place. A mistake
as I emerged this time,
that time and found the markers gone.

Oh, my darling, I have hidden
long in alien places
guarding treasures for someone

loyal to the game. But they say
you are bored with such memory,
that you, too, have grown up.

I'm Hiding
E.A. Markham

CRC

Susan

The crow drops the bone.
The bone rolls over the roof and jams tight in the gutter.
The crow fixes the bone with her eye and flaps away.

Do you think half a dead cow in a glass case is art, you
ask me, your face already set in opposition. I know my options:

(i) Concede that, yes, this particular example does
    challenge popular perceptions of art.

(ii) Shrug in a neutral, each-to-their-own sort of a way.

(iii) Attempt to defend art since Impressionism.

Shaw

Gently, gently. But I know my opinion and I feel my frustration.

The rain fills the gutter. Muck, moss and slipped-down slates block its way. Soon, water seeps over the rim, taking the bone with it and streaking my window with droppings of mud. The bone bounces from pavement to road.

The Animals exhibition is a puzzle of images that aren't how I think of animals. It keeps me awake at night. There's nothing so graphic as a sliced up cow; nothing so familiar as the furry faces in a wildlife documentary. I run the photographs through my head. A circus llama posing by a sheet of canvas, a giant poodle head with glassy eyes, four bears in a domestic tableau and a spare giraffe from the museum store. And then come the creatures in jars. The swollen face of a fruit bat crammed in over umbrella wings. A tiny polar bear bobbing in formaldehyde. I'm standing in the school laboratory, opening a cupboard on all the compelling and repellent specimens; breathing in the acrid yellow smell.

Crow spots the bone and swoops from chimney pot to kerb's edge.

In a darkened room there is a Dead Horse, all shiny and brown like a new conker. In the stilled video it is caught mid air, legs springing and buckling from the impact of the stun gun. The lens sways rhythmically over the frozen image; gently, gently rocking on a clatter of hoof beats. I stay with

SUSAN SHAW

the horse, caught up in the loop of repetition and reluctant to leave.

Crow fits her bill around the squat, grey knuckle of bone; flaps upwards and disappears on frayed black wings.

Redefining the relationship between animals and humans, reads the exhibition text. Freezing is the word inside my head.

I'm not really interested in animals, you say, eager for the coffee shop, I don't have anything to do with them.

Except.

Except for every dog that squats outside your door. All those scuttlers and creepers beetling in from outside. The shrill summer flies and whining wasps you swat. Pieces of muscle, blood, fat and bone disguised in supermarket packages. The cat that scoops and fills your borders. Rabbits that go thud and bump under your tyres. Tiny mites rooted in your eyelashes and trawling through the fridge. Your silky smooth leopard print slip.

On the roof top, there's a place where the slates slope down, angling into a leaded joint with the chimney stack. Here, crow stashes her hardened crusts, broken bones and bacon rind. From the sky she scours bird tables and back yards; roadsides and rubbish dumps.

From an aerial perch, her voice vibrates down through the house.

Every morning.

Lady? Lady?

Will you scratch my back please?

It's terribly itchy

and I can't reach it....

Oh, just there, that's right....

Oh yes....

Don't stop....

Don't stop now lady....

Longer and harder....

Oh that's lovely....   Don't stop.

Um, that's my bus.   Sorry.

Oh OK.... Lady?

Will you scratch my back?

Please?

[an old woman at a bus stop]

Man in Age
Tony Williams

Guiltily, his children
Visit him, suppose he's
Lonely, which he is. They
Bring their children and their
Memories, but not his,

Which he has tried to put
Away; but daily the day
Reminds him of every
Week. He's lonely. Now then,
Dad. He tries not to speak.

NEW RHYMES FOR THE NURSERY

Tony Williams

The charity workers at rush hour spill
Down the avenued rat-run of Hanover Hill
It's five for a squirrel and ten for a kill
And none of it's told in the tales from Grimm

When absent through illness he misses his chance
To shield his lover from dirty romance
As under the underpass drunken they dance
And none of it's told in the tales from Grimm

A note on the table tells somebody's kid
That he'll get a reward for the things that were did
He eats up his dinner and keeps it all hid
And none of it's told in the tales from Grimm

The jeweller works at his intricate flash
To worry the king from his commoner's rash
It's good but it's thrown on the throne-room to smash
And none of it's told in the tales from Grimm

A sexual act on a council estate
Aborted through conscience. The hour is late
As they walk hand in hand to a seventy-eight
And none of it's told in the tales from Grimm

Urban investitures. Shocking reports
Of teenagers having a hand down their shorts
Laughed at by parents, ignored by the courts
And none of it's told in the tales from Grimm

Some horrible news as a seasonal gift
A lover found dead after taking a lift
When left on the motorway after a rift
And none of it's told in the tales from Grimm

The businessmen bray like a gang on the hunt
As one of them picks on a girl for a stunt
She solemnly swoons for the quarrelsome cunt
And none of it's told in the tales from Grimm

The window pane shatters. A stranger falls back
On a piss-riddled blanket and begs for some crack
He softens his voice as he changes his tack
And none of it's told in the tales from Grimm

The streets are bereft in the barrelling rain
The timetables say that a stuttering train
Is travelling by. God is insane,
And none of it's told in the tales from Grimm

A girl with a past and a tear in her frock
Is shovelling gravel off Immingham dock
The fish in the harbour gulp plummeting rock
And none of it's told in the tales from Grimm

Hello!

Hello....

Nice day isn't it?

Oh, yes I'm glad to be out...

all the lovely flowers

and the sun shining.

Makes me glad to be alive...

you see...

it's hell at home.

72

[old man to passers-by in the park]

Home is where you make it.
Childhood is never outgrown; only, with determination,
adapted, reviewed, refined. Fear and wonder are constants.

Childhood is where you make it.
Determination is never outgrown; only with fear and wonder
adapted, reviewed, refined. Home is a constant.

Wonder is where you make it.
Home is never outgrown, only, with Childhood Fear, reviewed, refined,
adapted Determination is a

you is where Fear is never outgrown you Wonder you review you
make it refined with Childhood is constant you never make it Home is
Home is

this much

Home is where

bones grating against each other
black holes black   ho

      ho

      o

o

this is

this i s   *Janice Galloway*

there is

make up.

Mother's red lipstick on a crocheted mat.

This is my home.
say it is bright the bright one say

is it is constant
a

bright room with beige flowers. Tan leaves
and orange stripes. The same wallpaper on every wall. The
curtains are so white and you can see right through them
when it's sunny. Fibreglass. Fibre made of glass.When you
touch, they shock your fingers. Sometimes if you look hard,
really hard, you see the sparks. You try not to touch them
because of the shocks and because of the whiteness. You

need to be careful or you leave marks. Tell-tale marks. Breath on the window makes a bloom like dragon-breath on the clean pane. Your breath. Past those twin circles is outside with the washing line, scrubby grass; tattie shaws in irregular clumps on a patch of grey earth. Rhubarb and potatoes. Things you can eat. Sometimes there is a dog or a cat pushing at something near the bins. There is only dirt in between the visible leaves. At the front, though, there are rosebushes. Roses, dahlias, night-scented stock. Out on the porch in the dark, holding the snib back till your thumb knuckle goes white so it doesn't make a noise, you have seen the moon coming out behind cloud, inhaled the smell of them mixed with rain.

The washing throws shadows. Shifting shapes.

In front of the naked potato drills, jumpers wave their arms.

They would be stiff if it was winter, sprouting frost like hairs. They would hurt your fingers. Shadows reach for the window when they see you watching, change their minds. Clouds nose about the sky like strays. Shadows. Clouds.

Maybe it's not as light as you thought.

Maybe it's almost dark.

Dim grainy air so the posters you have tacked on the wall are just blots. You know who they are though, know what they must be from habit. Doris Day and the Beatles, The Man from UNCLE with his lips painted over in nailpolish so you can kiss him and he won't spoil. Elvis in some kind of American soldier uniform is so far into the shade you can only see the sheen on his teeth. The wardrobe and dressing

table look black. On top of the dresser, the ancient cylinder
of talc, a brush and comb set, bits of make-up glimmer as
though through murky water. Mother's make-up. Scarlet. It
makes your lips scar

> on a crocheted mat the mat is
> beige with a pink trim. The mirror.

Take your time.

The mirror.

The mirror is full of orange bedspread. It has
cigarette holes in, a frilly trim that trails down to the carpet
but you can't see the carpet. Orange quilted pillow slips. You
can't see any of these things. Turn round though. You turn
around and there they are, the colours less acid, tangible.
Beside the bed, the cabinet with mother's books inside, their
spines angled so you can't read them unless you move them
on purpose. You have moved them on purpose plenty of
times. Angelique, The Practical Home Doctor and TRUE
CRIMES magazine underneath. TRUE CRIMES has creases
on the cover and a scared woman running. You have no idea
what she is running away from but it will be something. You
have no doubt it's the right thing she's doing. You slide them
back as exactly as you can manage, replace the wing-topped
specs. Even after all this practice, it makes you uneasy,
putting them back and hoping you haven't left smears on
the lenses, a fingerprint. On the other side of the bed,

Alice Through the Looking Glass with plasticine stains on
the picture of Humpty Dumpty. His swollen belly or neck or
whatever it is is all torn off; it is eroded and smells funny.
It smells of being small, wearing plastic sandals and lint.
Green. The plasticine was green. There are jotters here too,
little ink footprints on the corners, marching off the edge.
They have nowhere to run. Whose jotters are these? These
are JANE's jotters. Her pencils have chew marks down to the
lead. Black graphite tips between her teeth. A sheet with the
beginnings of a story and hangs on one snapped sentence,
waiting. A drawing of a tree with no leaves.

     Tv. There's tv on. A man's voice.

     It comes through the ceiling. THE ITHER
CHANNEL SADIE SWITCH ON THE OTHER YIN and a
comedy show comes on, laughing. They are up there walking
about over your head. These are your neighbours. They have
white hair. The light fittings flutter when they move. You've
been in this room a long time and the tv never gets any
quieter. Muttering, laughter, muttering, applause and catcalls.
Cat. Calls. They start too. You never get the jokes. Look at
the ca

     rpet. No-
           body
           is down
           there.

     There is nobody down there.
     You can jump on the floor all night and disturb

nothing. No-one will tell you to stop. Unless. Unless they
look in. In the corner of the room next to the single sheets
of piano score, your sensible straps, a hairnet bunched in on
itself like a dead spider and n

      othing in the far corner of the room, a
brass fruit bowl with n
      othing

      But you can't keep from looking at it forever.
      You can't pretend it's not there.

      A fire vent over the bedhead, its handle, waiting
open or shut the grille. It glints like teeth in the dark, makes
a sound like sore bones. You don't want to get any closer but
it is coming anyway, sidling up. Without wanting to, you lift
your eyes to the s-shaped slits. Draw your eye to the beautiful
moulded rims. Look. Careful of dust, blown-back soot, the
smell of burning, look. It is

      thick orange and green brocade
      a sound
      less

      this is my home my
      home the

      place where I live with my mummy lives my

mummy and my big sister and my

h

o

me is a

room with no door.

Just a curtain at the top of a stairwell over a close.
The single window overlooks a brown street, shops. A barber's
with a blood-striped lance juts from the opposite wall, a
plain brown window with the name VIRGINIA in gold on
a navy ground. A woman's name. VIRGINIA. Over the
roofs, gulls. The sky is gunboat grey even at this time in
the afternoon. Salt deposits on the glass. Marks like dried
spit. This is your home.

Home your house this is where you live.

Turn.

A red divan so close to the window recess it needs
pushed aside to get past. It goes wall to wall, back to the
light. There are spots through the redness if you concentrate,
different colours yellow ochre, olive green, steel blue,
albino-flesh white, circled with a thin line of grainy black.
Like fish eyes. Move around the divan frame and they do
too, following. There are two sides to this room. This is one.
It is full of the divan. If it was opened it would fill almost

the whole place but it is never opened till night and even
then there is still enough room to watch tv. The tv. It's on
the other side, perching on a side-table, still close enough to
touch. It might even be on. Test Card: black and white
squares and a medley of Scottish Military Airs. Pipes and
drums. You've watched it before, waiting for something to
come on. Sometimes something does. Next to it is the
fireplace, swirly tiles and a green rug with two burn holes
where live coals have fallen. The holes have a weal round
the outside, like a crater, something off a picture of the moon
or where pus has oozed out of your face only the edges are
hard. They scratch. Fire burns round holes. Perfect ellipses.
Over the fire – it is not on, the grate is swept – there is the
bakelite radio, the copper-colour alarm clock, the brass of
Queen Elizabeth I in a down-to-the-floor dress and a ruff
round her neck her eyes blank like a vampire and two
porcelain people in Arcadian costumes. They are all on the
mantelpiece. The porcelain maybe it is china. It breaks. It isn't
broken but it breaks keep away don't touch. It is a man and
a woman turned away from each other she has a half-opened
fan and half-smile and he has knee-breeches and a tricorn
hat, hands out-turned like an Indian dancer. Cocky. White
faces and rosebud mouths

     like
     like
     remember the time you found the mouse under
the sink in a trap its nose turned up like it just smelled
something nice to eat only its spine got snapped instead

nobody told you not to look under there maybe they thought
it was ok you would never find it so you didn't tell just you
got sick but nothing came up thinking about its whiskers
sticking up that way as though it was looking for something
good and this trap with the spring, loaded and waiting for it
in the dark when it was distracted by a promise. Snap. Snap.
It was lucky you didn't get a row they didn't find out. Maybe
it's in there now. Behind the wee cream-coloured doors
under the sink.

Through the gap in the wall, look and see.

The cream-coloured door, the red vegetable rack
and Baby Belling a two-ring Baby Belling it's called Baby
pretending to be a kitchenette. A pink potty is under there
somewhere, the inside all scoured from scrubbing, squint
on a pile of newspaper. That's what you were looking for
when you found the mouse. Don't look now. For now, it
doesn't matter.

The ceiling.
I don't know what colour the ceiling is.
Maybe I never looked at it. Maybe I listened.

Mother is under the floorboards. That noise is her,
moving about cleaning something. It could be anything.
She is not angry. You can tell from the cleaning sounds.
They are not too loud. Worn-smooth bouclé cloth of the
divan beneath bare legs, people's feet passing on the paving
outside, the odd car engine, weans shouting. The half-light

on the manilla coloured wallpaper and Dettol off the stairs
become one. Iodine, ancient fur coat, the acrid stink of dross
and matches waiting in the grate. Before it is completely
dark, mother's slipper soles will begin dragging like corpses
on the stone steps, coming cl

o

o

there is

make-up
mother's red lipstick on a crocheted mat

you can't keep from looking forever

Through the s-shaped slits, her eyes.
Her pupils are black holes.

Watching back.

THE SCREAM

Mary Bonner

When she had first come out on the balcony minutes before, a lifetime before, Liliana had shut her eyes in the late afternoon sun, breathing in its warmth, feeling it move across her arms and over her white T-shirt. It was great to be out of those thick tops. If her best friend Teresa could see she needed a bra, why couldn't Mamma? She couldn't wear sweatshirts all summer, she'd roast. She was secretly pleased when the boys at school first started to giggle like kids and laugh behind her back, although she was embarrassed too. They had another reason to talk behind her back now. She heard the names, as she was meant to, infame, infame. She couldn't ask Mamma for a bra now. She had enough to do with Pino and Assunta, but all the same, she might have noticed. Nonna would help, but she'd dig her fingers into her as if she was a piece of fruit at the market. Maybe Mrs Giuliano? Liliana knew Teresa envied her woman's body, but Liliana would give anything to be in her place; Teresa still had her Papa with her. One two, one two.

There was a hum of cars like sleepy insects, buzzing below. A line of Mr Giuliano's best work shirts were flapping on next-door's balcony. Mrs Giuliano would bring them in just before her husband came home. Perhaps she could ask her today, after Mamma and Nonna left to visit Papa. Should she? After the other day? She'd see. Mamma said Mrs

Giuliano wore too much lipstick. But Liliana liked her. She saved Liliana the free samples of eye shadows and mascara that came with her magazines. She kept them, away from Mamma, in her middle drawer, right at the back. One two, one two.

She was still leaning over the balcony, clenching the long string which tied her to the basket - letting her nails stay rooted in the fleshy part of her right hand. Mamma was going to put the shopping in there for supper. She had gone with Nonna, first to the market around the corner, finishing with Mr Ribisi's across the street. They didn't normally take long, even though Nonna insisted on pressing all the oranges with her rough bony fingers and holding up the aubergines to the sun.

Now Papa was gone, the market traders tried to palm them off with rotten fruit and not give Nonna what she had chosen. But Nonna always insisted.

"Have you forgotten Giuseppi, that Francesco used his own money as a favour to you, when you couldn't afford to pay?" Her whisper one day was like a cat hissing. "He never told. Not even Ninu."

Giuseppi would shove the fruit at Nonna without looking at her but when they got home they'd find extra fresh limes or oranges. Liliana burnt with embarrassment when Nonna made a scene. She hated Papa then; it was all his fault. But she couldn't help admiring how Nonna stood up to the traders, pointing her black-sleeved skinny arm at them like a branch in the wind.

Before all this trouble about Papa, the traders always made a fuss of Nonna and of her too. When Liliana was very young, they crouched down to her and patted her head. Nonna was rude though, always in a rush, not even having time to accept the treats they offered. Mamma was just as bad. Now, the traders looked at her sullenly - even Giuseppi, who had only just started winking at her. Their mouths were clamped tight as if their jaws had been wired together like her front teeth. They scared her and she was glad then of her thick tops. When they left the market Nonna would put a hand on Liliana's arm and grip it tight.

"Walk proud, Liliana," she'd hiss. "We have nothing to be ashamed of. Your Papa has come to his senses at last."

When she said 'at last' it was a sigh, as if it was too late already.

One two, one two. She was still waiting. She had already played her game to see how far she could swing the basket. Today she had done well. On the right, she had got it level with the boy who annoyed Mr Ribisi by selling water-melons near his shop - and on the left it had almost been in line with the corner of the farmacia two doors down. Then it was time to see how long it would move on its own. Thirteen complete swings was her record. One....two...three... But she'd stopped counting. Her body was crying out. Her arm ached from the effort of holding the basket and all this waiting. The basket lost its gentle rocking motion. For a moment it dangled clumsily, scuffing into other balconies, jarring against the rails. Pain shot through her arm like an injection. Tightening her grip on the string, she clawed back one, two handfuls, pulling its roughness through her fingers as she raised the basket. Under control again, it resumed its sleepily creaking sideways motion. One two, one two.

Inside the apartment Pino and Assunta had been arguing over what to watch on television. Then she heard Assunta laugh - her little hiccuping giggle which sometimes turned her face pink and made her hold her tummy in with her small hands as if it would crack open. Pino was a charmer, with his crinkly eyes and mischievous smile. Mamma's tesoro. He made Liliana laugh too, sometimes. But he could be a pain – especially when he got upset about Papa and banged his fists so heavily on the kitchen table that her knife rattled on her plate. That was silly. But Pino still climbed into her bed at night, long after he was supposed to be asleep, and she would curl her body around the small warm ball of her brother. He woke up crying every time he wet the bed. "It doesn't matter Pino," she'd say. "It doesn't matter tesoro." They all missed Papa. But they would be with him soon. Mamma had promised. "A new start," she had said.

Liliana enjoyed the quiet. Mamma only asked her to wait on the balcony with the basket when she was in a hurry – usually just before she left to see Papa. Mamma normally gave her a quick little smile to show that everything was OK, but her eyes would dart all over the place as if they were looking for something. More of Mamma's hair was turning grey. It looked as if a spider's web had fallen on it. She hadn't dyed it for weeks. She didn't have time. That's why, the other day, she hadn't told Mamma about her ripped school skirt and blouse.

"I'll do it for you," Mrs Giuliano said after Liliana burst into tears on the balcony.

"They, they…" Liliana almost burnt her throat when she tried to swallow. "They say Papa is, is a – " If only Teresa had been at school that day.

"I know why they did it." Mrs Giuliano sounded impatient as she reached across. "It's only the side seams. I'll leave them here for you tonight. Don't tell anyone."

That night Liliana found the clothes mended and neatly folded. She heard raised voices between Mrs Giuliano and her husband. They never normally argued. She peered at the night sky, tears rolling down her cheeks.

Two women had been regular visitors since Papa was away. Liliana recognised the older one. She thought she had been to her house ages ago. It was white, like a palace, somewhere near the mountains. There'd been a big party. But she had never gone back. Mamma and Papa had argued about it but Mamma had stood firm. "It's bad enough as it is, without you glorying in it," she told him.

The women made a big fuss of Pino, pulling stupid smiley faces at him and lifting him onto their laps like fishermen hauling up their catch, but he still ran screaming to Mamma even though he normally liked attention. The older woman had a hooked nose and wore gold necklaces and bracelets. She was still ugly. Mamma always looked so worried when they came, like a bird trapped indoors. The last time, the older woman did most of the talking. Her words sounded kind but Liliana wasn't fooled.

"Bernardo and Salvatore send their best wishes. They want to know if you need anything."

Mamma had sent her out of the room with Pino after that. Liliana thought she remembered Bernardo from the big house. He had soft fat fingers. Never did an honest day's work in his life, Mamma said.

The visitors hadn't been back for two weeks. Mamma must have frightened them off. After they'd left Liliana had heard Mamma and Nonna talk about it.

"Did they offer money again?"

Mamma hesitated. "They said they could help if we're struggling. Said it must be hard being married to an infame. They were very sympathetic." Mamma sounded like a horse snorting.

"What are you going to do?" said Nonna. There was silence. Liliana couldn't hear the spoon gently scraping the pan. Nonna must be tasting the sauce to see if it needed more oregano. "We should get the police to move us, as they wanted to in the first place."

"Francesco wants us to stay close -"

"Carmela! Francesco has the carabinieri with him all the time. Who do we have? No-one."

"Maybe." Mamma sounded unsure.

"There's no choice. He's not playing the big man anymore. Him and his family! I wish you'd never -"

"Mamma! Enough!"

"I should have made you listen to your Papa. He knew Francesco's kind would bring heartbreak."

There was silence. Nonna's voice was very quiet. "Carmela, you can tell the children to wash their hands, the food is ready."

Liliana had got Assunta and Pino sat around the table for at least five minutes before Nonna and Mamma came out. They had both been crying.

One two, one two. Liliana liked the weight of the shopping and the effort it took to pull up. She knew that when she started to take in her haul, Pino and Assunta would dash out and fight like hungry birds over who would hold the string. Assunta always won because she was older. But she'd draw herself up to her full height, flick off an imaginary speck of grit from her brother's cheek, and with a serious look on her face, hand over the string to Pino.

Liliana saw Uncle Ninu first. She put up her left hand to wave to him. She started to smile and almost called out. He hadn't been around for ages. The last time he visited Papa - with one of Papa's friends - there had been a big row. Uncle Ninu had stormed out of the apartment without looking back. He had said some bad things like 'infame' - traitor, but he'd been angry. Mamma and Papa stayed up that night talking in whispers and sometimes Mamma had cried. Liliana had padded out of her room to listen and heard Papa say it would be for the best.

"It's the only way." Papa sounded worried.

"Speak against your family? You could do that?"

"I can't face prison. It's not me the police want anyway. Extortion is just a side issue. They want the main operation." Liliana didn't know what extortion meant. But it sounded serious.

"The police will protect us?"

"New identities, new home, money every month. They promised. It will be a fresh start after the trial."

"Ninu was mad. He didn't believe you were just questioned. What about Bernardo? Salvatore?"

"Ninu's always talked tough but he'll calm down. Bernardo and Salvatore will just lie low for a while. Ninu won't let anything happen to you or the children. Liliana's his special girl, after all." Papa sounded like he was trying to smile, like he did when he was hiding a present for them behind his back.

"I'm scared Francesco. I want so much to leave this life but – "

"Sh, cara," he whispered. "It will be all right. I have such plans for us. It's my chance to make things right, move out from Ninu's shadow at last."

The next day they said nothing was wrong and never once mentioned they'd all have to move somewhere else. That made her angry. She was not stupid.

One two, one two. When she was little, Uncle Ninu used to throw her up in the air when she ran to him. It always made Mamma cross when he did this. He always told Liliana how pretty she was and that she'd grow up to be beautiful. She would say something which made him laugh and he'd throw back his head and let the sound pour out. She liked his laugh, it was big and kind, just like him. She missed it. Today Uncle Ninu looked up but did not smile. He quickly looked away. She didn't know why. Not then.

She heard the shots – although at first she didn't realise what they were. They sounded like explosions. Uncle Ninu had pointed a gun. Nonna was lying face down on the ground. Motionless. Her body was twisted with her right arm stretched in front of her as if she was trying to reach for something. Her hand still clutched at the handles of her bag which had burst open – spilling out oranges and melons which lolled into the road. Beads of glass from shattered bottles glinted like jewels in the blood which spread out from under Nonna; olive oil oozed across the street and Nonna's dress was twisted up her legs, showing part of her thighs. Liliana had expected Mamma to run out of the shop but instead out came Papa's friend looking frightened. Then they ran. Past the shop, down the street, across the road and out of sight. Mamma? Mamma?

For one, maybe two seconds afterwards, there was silence in the piazza. Total and complete. That was before the scream. Before Liliana was fully aware that the basket was still swinging below her. One two, one two. It creaked as it moved on its string, which she still held tight in her hand.

If she had thought about it, really thought about it, she'd know it reminded her of the noise Nonna's chair made when she'd last snuggled onto Papa's lap – even though Mamma had said she was too old. She hadn't felt too old and she and Papa had rocked backwards and forwards, backwards and forwards, creaking, as he teased her about Giuseppi. It was also the sound of floorboards cracking when you tried to listen to what Mamma and Papa were saying when they sat up late at night, or how the hinges squeak when the shutters were blown by the breeze if Nonna had forgotten to hook them back properly. One two, one two. The sound was like all these familiar things. Her mind bumped into them as it was dragged along by what she had just seen and heard.

The basket slowed to a gentle lullaby motion, one two, one two. Her mouth shuddered open. First there was silence and then the scream was wrenched out of her like an animal clawing at her throat. One two, one two.

Sentence

Don Barnard

Names were the first dropped stitches of self
in her unravelling, so he peopled all
her sentences with guesses and she laughed,
but left more and more half-said, as the cells
unlocked, unlocked in her emptying head's whimsical
slow paroling of words, and then the questions,
asked and answered endlessly – "Where's Jim?"
"I'm Jim." "Oh yes!... Where's Jim?" – and what hurt most,
her long wordless howls and her silences,
for she was leaving him, slipping through gaps
in herself while he cleaned shit, undressed and dressed
and tea-spooned life through slack, unwilling lips,
coping still and telling her her name,
hoping for that as her last word, when it came.

Watching American Beauty

Tracey O'Rourke

Her kisses are red petals he pulls from his mouth
attar of roses floods the gap unfolding
in our lives between the seen and the imagined
a plain-day impossibility – and truth's not there.
Still, we sit in the vast and private darkness
strangely alive and alone as her clothes
slip away in a fretful passacaglia
of desire. And who owns the gasp?
the whispered hosanna from another mouth
somewhere out there as her rosebud
breasts reveal a girlish self-deception.
How our breath hovers from him to her
Caught in the moment before the moment
of possession – where there is still going back.

Soft. Kind and soft.

Yes. She's so much better when she has a boyfriend.

[one man to another in a bar]

The Universal Story

Ali Smith

There was a man dwelt by a churchyard.

Well, no, okay, it wasn't always a man; in this particular case it was a woman. There was a woman dwelt by a churchyard.

Though, to be honest, nobody uses that word much nowadays. Everybody says cemetery. And nobody really says dwelt anymore. In other words:

There was once a woman who lived by a cemetery. Every morning when she woke up she looked out of her back window and saw –

Actually, no. There was once a woman who lived by – no, in – a second-hand bookshop. She lived in the flat on the first floor and ran the shop which took up the whole of downstairs. There she sat, day after day, among the skulls and the bones of second-hand books, the stacks and shelves of them spanning the lengths and breadths of the long and narrow rooms, the piles of them swaying up, precarious like rootless towers, towards the cracked plaster of the ceiling. Though their bent or riffled or still-chaste spines had been bleached by years of anonymous long-gone light, each of them had been new once, bought in a bookshop full of the shine of other new books. Now each was here, with too many possible reasons to guess at when it came to the question of how it had ended up sunk in the bookdust which specked the air in which the woman, on this winter's day, sat by herself, sensing all round her the weight of it, the covers shut on so many millions of pages that might never be opened to light again.

The shop was down a sidestreet off the centre of a small rural village which few tourists visited in the summer and in which business had slowed considerably since 1982, the year the Queen Mother, looking frail and holding her hat on her head with one hand because of the wind, had cut the ribbon on the bypass which made getting to the city much quicker and stopping in the village quite difficult. Then the bank had closed, and eventually the post office. There was a grocers, but most people drove to the supermarket six miles away. The supermarket also stocked books, though hardly any.

Occasionally someone would come into the second-hand bookshop looking for something he or she had heard about on the radio or read about in the papers. Usually the woman in the shop would have to apologise for not having it. For instance, it was February now. Nobody had been into the shop for four days. Occasionally a bookish teenage girl or boy, getting off the half past four school-bus which went between the village and the town, used to push, shy, at the door of the shop and look up with the kind of delight you can see even from behind, in the shoulders and back and the angle of head of a person looking up at the endless promise of books. But this hadn't happened for a while.

The woman sat in the empty shop. It was late afternoon. It would be dark soon. She watched a fly in the window. It was early in the year for flies. It flew in veering triangles, then settled on The Great Gatsby by F. Scott Fitzgerald, to bask in what late winter sun there was.

Or – no. Wait:

There was once a fly resting briefly on an old paperback book in a second-hand bookshop window. It had paused there in a moment of warmth before launching back into the air, which it would do any second now. It wasn't any special or unusual kind of fly, or a fly with an interesting species-name – for instance a robber fly or an assassin fly, a bee fly or a thick-headed fly, a dance fly, a dagger fly, a snipe fly or a down-looker fly. It wasn't even a stout or a cleg or a midge. It was a common house fly, a musca domesticus linnaeus, of the diptera family, which means it had two wings. It stood on the cover of the book and breathed air through its spiracles.

It had been laid as an egg less than a millimetre long in a wad of manure in a farmyard a mile and a half away, and had become a legless maggot, feeding off the manure it had been laid in. Then, because winter was coming, it had wriggled by sheer muscle contraction nearly a hundred and twenty feet. It had lain dormant for almost four months in the grit round the base of a wall under several feet of stacked hay in the barn. In a spell of mild weather over the last weekend it had broken the top off the pupa and pulled itself out, a fly now, six millimetres long. Under an eave of the barn it had spread and dried its wings and waited for its body to harden in the unexpectedly spring-like air coming up from the Balearics. It had entered the rest of the world through a fly-sized crack in the roof of the barn that morning, then zigzagged for over a mile looking for light, warmth and food. When the woman who owned the shop had opened the kitchen window to let the condensation out as she cooked her lunch, it had flown in. Now it was

excreting and regurgitating, which is what flies do when
they rest on the surfaces of things.

To be exact, it wasn't an it, it was a female fly, with a
longer body and red slitted eyes set wider apart than if she
had been a male fly. Her wings were each a thin, perfect,
delicately-veined membrane. She had a grey body and six
legs, each with five supple joints, and she was furred all
over her legs and her body with tiny bristles. Her face was
striped velvet-silver. Her long mouth had a sponging end
for sucking up liquid and for liquefying solids like sugar or
flour or pollen.

She was sponging with her proboscis the picture of
the actors Robert Redford and Mia Farrow on the cover of
the Penguin 1974 edition of The Great Gatsby. But there
was little there really of interest, as you might imagine, to
a house fly which needs urgently to feed and to breed,
which is capable of carrying over one million bacteria and
transmitting everything from common diarrhoea to
dysentery, salmonella, typhoid fever, cholera, poliomyelitis,
anthrax, leprosy and tuberculosis; and which senses that at
any moment a predator will catch her in its web or crush
her to death with a fly-swat; or if she survives these that it
will still, any moment now, simply be cold enough to snuff
out herself and all ten of the generations she is capable of
setting in motion this year, all nine hundred of the eggs she
will be capable of laying given the chance, the average

twenty days of life of an average common house fly.

No. Hang on. Because:

There was once a 1974 Penguin edition of F. Scott Fitzgerald's classic American novel, The Great Gatsby, in the window of a quiet second-hand book shop in a village that very few people visited any more. It had a hundred and eighty-eight numbered pages and was the twentieth Penguin edition of this particular novel – it had been reprinted three times in 1974 alone; this popularity was partly due to the film of the novel which came out that year, directed by Jack Clayton. Its cover, once bright yellow, had already lost most of its colour before it arrived at the shop. Since the book had been in the window it had whitened even more. In the film-still on it, ornate in a twenties-style frame, Robert Redford and Mia Farrow, the stars of the film, were also quite faded, though Redford was still dapper in his golf cap, and Farrow, in a very becoming floppy hat, suited the sepia effect that the movement of sun and light on the glass had brought to her quite by chance.

The novel had first been bought for 30p (6/) in 1974 in a Devon bookshop by Rosemary Child, who was twenty-two, and who had felt the urge to read the book before she saw the film. She married her fiancé Roger two years later. They mixed their books and gave their doubles to a Cornwall hospital. This one had been picked off the hospital library trolley in Ward 14 one long hot July afternoon in 1977 by

Sharon Patten, a fourteen-year-old girl with a broken hip who was stuck in bed in traction and bored because Wimbledon was over. Her father had seemed pleased at visiting-hour when he saw it on her locker, and though she'd given up reading it halfway through she kept it there by the waterjug for her whole stay and smuggled it home with her when she was discharged. Three years later, when she didn't care anymore what her father thought of what she did, she gave it to her school-friend David Connor who was going to university to do English, telling him it was the most boring book in the world. David read it. It was perfect. It was just like life is. Everything is beautiful, everything is hopeless. He walked to school quoting bits of it to himself under his breath. By the time he went up north to university in Edinburgh two years later, now a mature eighteen-year-old, he admired it, as he said several times in the seminar, though he found it a little adolescent and believed the underrated Tender Is The Night to be Fitzgerald's real masterpiece. The tutor, who every year had to mark around a hundred and fifty abysmal first year essays on The Great Gatsby, nodded sagely and gave him a high pass in his exam. In 1985, having landed a starred first and a job in Personnel Management, David sold all his old literature course books to a girl called Mairead for thirty pounds. Mairead didn't like English – it had no proper answers – and decided to do economics instead. She sold them all again, making a lot more money than David had. The Great Gatsby went for £2.00, six times its original price, to a first year student called Gillian Edgbaston. She managed never to read it and left it on the shelves of the rented house she'd been living in when she moved out in 1990. Brian Jackson, who owned the rented house, packed it in a box which sat behind the freezer in his garage for five years. In 1995 his mother Rita came to visit and while he was tidying out his garage she found it in the open box, just lying there on the gravel in his driveway. The Great Gatsby! she said. She hadn't read it for years. He remembers her reading it that summer, it was two summers before she died, and her feet were up on the sofa and her head was deep in the book. She had a whole roomful of books at home. When she died in 1997 he boxed them all up and gave them to a registered charity. The registered charity checked through them for what was valuable and sold the rest on, in auctioned boxes of thirty miscellaneous paperbacks, a fiver per box, to second hand shops all over the country.

The woman in the quiet second-hand bookshop had opened the box she bought at auction and had raised her eyebrows, tired. Another Great Gatsby.

Penguin Modern Classics. F. Scott Fitzgerald. Now a Major Film. The book was in the window. Its pages and their edges were dingy yellow because of the kind of paper used in old Penguin Modern Classics; by nature these books won't last. A fly was resting on the book now in the weak sun in the window.

But the fly suddenly swerved away into the air, because a man had put his hand in among the books in the window display in the second-hand bookshop and was picking the book up.

Now :

There was once a man who reached his hand in and picked a second-hand copy of F. Scott Fitzgerald's The Great Gatsby out of the window of a quiet second-hand bookshop in a small village. He turned the book over as he went to the counter.

How much is this one, please? he asked the grey-looking woman.

She took it from him and checked the inside cover.

That one's £1, she said.

It says thirty pence here on it, he said, pointing to the back.

That's the 1974 price, the woman said.

The man looked at her. He smiled a beautiful smile. The woman's face lit up.

But, well, since it's very faded, she said, you can have it for fifty.

Done, he said.

Would you like a bag for it? she asked.

No, it's okay, he said. Have you any more?

Any more Fitzgerald? the woman said. Yes, under F. I'll just —

No, the man said. I mean, any more copies of The Great Gatsby.

You want another copy of The Great Gatsby? the woman said.

I want all your copies of it, the man said, smiling.

The woman went to the shelves and found him four more copies of The Great Gatsby. Then she went through to the storeroom at the back of the shop and checked for more.

Never mind, the man said. Five'll do. Two pounds for the lot, what do you say?

His car was an old Mini Metro. The back seat of it was under a sea of different editions of The Great Gatsby. He cleared some stray copies from beneath the driver's seat so they wouldn't slide under his feet or the pedals while he was driving, and threw the books he'd just bought over his shoulder on to the heap without even looking. He started the engine. The next second-hand bookshop was six miles away, in the city. His sister had called him from her bath two Fridays ago. James, I'm in the bath, she'd said. I need F Scott Fitzgerald's The Great Gatsby.

F what's the what? he'd said.

She told him again. I need as many as possible, she said.

Okay, he'd said.

He worked for her because she paid well; she had a grant.

Have you ever read it? she asked.

No, he'd said. Do I have to?

So we beat on, she'd said. Boats against the current. Borne back ceaselessly into the past. Get it?

What about petrol money, if I'm supposed to drive all over the place looking for books? he'd said.

You've got five hundred quid to buy five hundred books. You get them for less, you can keep the change. And I'll pay you two hundred on top for your trouble. Boats against the current. It's perfect, isn't it?

And petrol money? he'd said.

Included, she'd sighed.

Because:

There was once a woman in the bath who had just phoned her brother and asked him to find her as many copies of The Great Gatsby as possible. She shook the drips off the phone, dropped it over the side on to the bathroom carpet and put her arm back into the water, quick, because it was cold.

She was collecting the books because she made full-sized boats out of things boats aren't usually made out of. Three years ago she had made a three-foot long boat out of daffodils which she and her brother had stolen, at night, from people's front gardens all over town. She had launched it, climbing into it, in the local canal. Water had come up round her feet almost immediately, then up round her ankles, her knees, her thighs, till she was midriff-deep in icy water and daffodils floating all round her, unravelled.

But a small crowd had gathered to watch it sink and the story had attracted a lot of local and even some national media attention. Sponsored by Interflora, which paid enough for her to come off unemployment benefit, she made another boat, five foot long and out of mixed flowers, everything from lilies to snowdrops. It also sank, but this time was filmed for an arts project, with her in it, sinking. This had won her a huge arts commission to make more unexpected boats. Over the last two years she had made ten- and twelve-footers out of sweets, leaves, clocks and photographs, and had launched each one with great ceremony at a different UK port. None of them had lasted more than eighty feet out to sea.

The Great Gatsby, she thought in the bath. It was a book she remembered from her adolescence, and as she'd been lying in the water fretting about what to do next so her grant wouldn't be taken away from her, it had suddenly come into her head.

It was perfect, she thought, nodding to herself. So we beat on. The last line of the book. She ducked her shoulders under the water to keep them warm.

And so, since we've come to the end already:

The seven-foot boat made of copies of The Great Gatsby stuck together with waterproof sealant was launched in the spring, in the port of Felixstowe.

The artist's brother collected over three hundred copies
of The Great Gatsby, and drove between Wales and Scotland
doing so. It is still quite hard to buy a copy of The Great
Gatsby second-hand in some of the places he visited. It cost
him a hundred and eighty three pounds fifty exactly. He kept
the change. He was also a man apt to wash his hands before
he ate, so was unharmed by any residue left by the fly earlier
in the story on the cover of the copy he bought in the quiet
second-hand bookshop.

This particular copy of The Great Gatsby, with the
names of some of the people who had owned it inked under
each other in their different handwritings on its inside first
page – Rosemary Child, Sharon Patten, David Connor, Rita
Jackson – was glued into the prow of the boat, which stayed
afloat for three hundred yards before it finally took in water
and sank.

The fly which had paused on the book that day spent
that evening resting on the light fitting and hovering more
than five feet above ground level. This is what flies tend to
do in the evenings. This fly was no exception.

The woman who ran the second-hand bookshop had been
delighted to sell all her copies of The Great Gatsby at once,
and to such a smiling young man. She replaced the one which
had been in the window with a copy of Dante's Divine Comedy,
and as she was doing so she fanned open the pages of the
book. Dust flew off. She blew more dust off the top of the

pages, then wiped it off her counter. She looked at the book-dust smudged on her hand. It was time to dust all the books, shake them all open. It would take her well into the spring. Fiction, then non-fiction, then all the sub-categories. Her heart was light. That evening she began, at the letter A.

The woman who lived by a cemetery, remember, back at the very beginning? She looked out of her window and she saw – Ah, but that's another story.

And lastly, what about the first, that man we began with, the man dwelt by a churchyard?

He lived a long and happy and sad and very eventful life, for years and years and years, before he died.

Oranges in his Pockets

L.V. O'Reilly

Saturdays
and Dempseys daschund van
bellied its way round,
weighing stones, pounds and ounces,
a travelling orchard-farm. Habitual
of the Saturday bath,
we queued up one behind one,
while Dempsey's Ma, in overcoat and half
gloves scribbled in pencil, her voice
ready rubbed, she'd tally up.
"That'll be three and six, for jaysas sake,
fix me up next week".
Big Christy would tease us,
like Brother Buck
and the High Chaparral, pigskin gloved,
acre span he tousled my sister's fire
brand hair – "Mad Jack" he'd say
then he'd laugh a belly laugh

as gripped in one hand she was a carasoule
amid neopolitan layers – Pinks, best whites,
and hard headed swedes.
Gleaner-limbed we carried fruits
and veg into bath-time. Galvanised grey stone
my Granda and his daughter carted
the upturned bath from our back yard.
Through the scullery pots of water
rotating on a four-ring gas.
it was two in, two out,
until all six of us glowed
like Mrs Dempsey's fruit bowl apples.
In flowered flannelette we sat on sanguine
red mocquette all Pippin and Golden Delicious.

II
Our Da said 'All the way from Seville'
one day a wooden box came,
and with every available pot and pan
segment, pith, peel, and juice were lobbed in.
A bathful in our front bedroom,
where the baby's cot sat
where we watched him wooden spoon stir
Under grease proof paper tarpaulin which,
on tip toe we lifted, dipped our fingers in and licked
and licked again.

Then come night, in bed, head to tail we imagined
fish and fish-scale next door, and smelled the smell
of citrus oceans, and played castanets of sounds -
mineola Clementine, Seville, mandarin, tangarine.
As mysterious as it came, one day when at school
it disappeared. The bath was scrubbed and hung,
but on Saturday when we sat in, there,
on the bottom was a thin film
the faintest hint of oranges "from Seville"
That was back then,
Now like a record spinning on a turntable
he repeats himself.
"Marmalade" he says to me,
That's a lovely word,
That's a lovely long word.
He says it laughing
As though some inner thread,
an out-of-plumb line
has him disconnected.
Like a lone globe he goes round and round.
"Jaysus would ye say it for me again,
Marmalade Da,
Sweet suffering Marmalade"
his voice fish trailing far off and deep.

Scuse me.

[man to woman on a crowded tube]

Ain't you got no manners.

Ain't you got no manners,

scuse me,

ain't you?

Ain't you got no manners?

Ain't you got no manners?

– *What?*

You just picked up my things

and chucked them.

What d'ya call that?

What d'ya call that?

What's that about?

– *Sorry.*

No.

You move.

You move from beside me.

Move from beside me right now.

You move.

Move from beside me.

Now.

Go on.

Move!

Allegra

Shelley Roche

'...And on the wall a marble tablet to be placed, with
these words:

In memory of
Allegra
daughter of G.G. Lord Byron
who died at Bagnacavallo, in Italy, April 20th, 1822,
Aged five years and three months.
'I shall go to her, but she shall not return to me'
2d Samuel, xii. 23'

I am pretty, lively
clean. People say
I shine
like the Milky Way.
Born in snow:
Cold that day
pressed gapingly
on the window pane

but could not have its way.
Saved and send for my Papa,
I ride with the ladies
tight in their brocades
fragrant
in their dusky skin.
We see chickens,
churches, sacks and men.

I must step
though I can run
and jump and do at home
with other ladies:
we eat sweet nuts
powder our faces.

There came a time plain ladies stopped me.
When Cold preyed on their empty rooms
and set my rose-gold hairs on end
they would pretend to study
though light had long grown grey.
Pale as turkey with its kisses

I let it have its way.
I touch fountains'
tiny coloured stones
at the bottom of their sea,
play tag in courtyard sun,
and my Papa,
I go to him
for he did not return to me

Billy

Bryony Doran

I shall call him Billy; a ninety-year-old child with a head as purple and transparent as an unfeathered fledgling. A man so frail, so elderly, he was an alien among us with large eye sockets and small head; prostrate on the pavement, tiny in his dark, pin-stripe suit. Big boots. I remember, he wore big, black boots. Proper, polished, work-man's boots.

Holding Billy's hand was a man in shorts. The man had a child with him, a boy of seven or eight wearing a Sheffield Wednesday shirt. The man crouched, the pavement digging into a bare knee, and held Billy's hand. Letting him cling tight.

A woman with short tinted hair, a cleaner at one of the local schools, I think, on the way to see her mother, knelt behind Billy. She stroked between his shoulder blades with one hand and cushioned his back from the pavement with the other. All the time speaking words. Soft, soothing, words of comfort.

Billy was on the pavement outside my house, well, just a little way along. I was going for a paper when someone shouted,

"Ring an ambulance will you, love?"

I saw the crown of an old head and people crouching. The woman on the phone asked me if he was an elderly gentleman. I should have asked 'Why', but I didn't, I said 'I think so.'

I rushed upstairs and got a blanket and a pillow, though it was a hot day and Billy had his pin-stripe suit on.

The man holding his hand said,

" I think he's warm enough."

"I've brought a pillow," I said.

The man shook his head.

"I've already put my travel rug under his head. I think he's okay, thanks."

He put his mouth close to Billy's ear.

"Can you hear me, love? What's your name?" He looked up at me, "Billy...I think he said... Billy."

I put the pillow and blanket on the bonnet of a car and crouched down at the back of Billy's head. There was a woman standing behind the man who held his hand. She had a wide flat face and shoulder length curly blonde hair. On her hip she balanced a young child. She had parked a grey jeep on the side street that ran up the hill behind us. It was her that had seen him fall. It was her who had got out of the jeep, leaving her child strapped in, and run to Billy, now quiet on the pavement.

"He just sort of crumpled," she said, "as he came down the hill. He seemed to be moving awful fast."

My legs were beginning to cramp, crouched there at the top of Billy's head. I felt helpless, scared, hoping he wouldn't die before the ambulance arrived. I had called the ambulance, as had a tall man in a royal blue shirt off for an early night out. I felt he was someone, maybe an ex-footballer, we should have recognised. He had stopped, parked his big car on the other side of the road and dialled 999 on his mobile phone.

We were held there suspended in time, whether by curiosity or compassion or a mixture of both, we had to stay. We had to wait for the ambulance. No-one knew Billy. We asked passers-by. They shook their heads. No-one had ever seen him in the club at the end of the road. I'd never seen him passing my window as I had seen other men; men suddenly retired and falling slowly every year into death. No one knew Billy, not even the cleaner lady, or Cyril who passed my window three or four times a day with his nearly-blind white stick and his cap and his 'getting away from the wife' walk.

Billy held his suited arms tight across his chest and when the man holding his hand tried to slip his free hand inside Billy's breast pocket, he seemed to pull them tighter; tight as a vice around his chest.

"What's your name, old lad? Is it Billy?"

Billy lay silent on the pavement. I could see all the fine veins on the top of his head; fine red and blue threads like the head of a foetus illuminated in the womb. Above his ear and on the top of his head were yellow encrustations where he must have knocked himself; the only sign that he might not have been cared for.

A group of kids gathered on the corner. I wanted to tell them to bugger off.

The man holding Billy's hand looked up,

"Clear off!" he mouthed, "Go on, get lost."

I looked at his son, who stood there on one leg,

"If you want to get off..." I said.

"No," he said, "I'll wait. The ambulance should be here soon."

It was a hot day at the end of August. Five o'clock in the afternoon. We were all in our summer clothes, except for Billy. The cleaner woman, on the way to see her mother, rubbed between Billy's shoulder blades.

"It's strange no-one knows him. What's he doing up here, and dressed so smart as well?"

The woman with the child on her hip frowned.

"I saw him coming up my street when I was still in the house. He was going at a fair old lick. He must have been lathered in those clothes, the street being so steep an' all."

"Where does that street go to?" asked the man holding Billy's hand.

The woman shook her head,

"Nowhere. Just the cemetery wall at the top, but you can't get through."

"Do you think he could have been going to a funeral?" I asked.

People passing in cars on their way home looked at us, gathered, crouching on the pavement.

The ambulance came up past the club, blue light silently flashing. No siren for Billy. I waved but they had already seen us;

a flock of sheep protecting the injured. Billy wouldn't let go of
the man's hand. He was still breathing, the ambulance man
established. We had already known that. They went and
fetched a metal trolley with wheels from the ambulance.
They turned the wheels so that they locked and between
them they lifted Billy, eyes still closed, light as a child, onto
the trolley.

"Can I have me hand back, mate?" the man asked.

Billy let go, eyes still kept tight shut. The cleaner woman
shook her squashed hand. The gravel from the pavement has
pressed holes into the back of her fingers. The ambulance
men shut the doors. No one got in the back with Billy. We
all shook our heads when they asked if anyone knew him.

The tartan rug lay folded into a pillow on the pavement.
The man who had been holding Billy's hand picked it up.
It was sodden with blood, soaked through to the pavement.

"Get us a plastic bag from the car, lad," he said to his
son. The boy brought back an insulated freezer bag. I knew
it was the wrong one.

"I'll get you a bag," I said.

"No, it doesn't matter," the man said, putting the blanket
in the bag, trying not to touch the blood.

"Would you like to come in and wash your hands?"

The man looks at me, slightly suspicious.

"No, I'll be alright."

"Would you like me to put the bag in my wheely bin?"

"If you don't mind."

The gathering split. Going once again in invisible directions. I put the blanket in the empty wheely bin and, for a week, every time I went to the bin, I thought of Billy, and his blood lying in the bottom.

I didn't want a dog licking Billy's blood off the pavement so I filled a bowl with warm water and washing up suds and splashed it onto the spot. It stayed. A sticky mass which over the days turned to a dark brown stain on the pavement.

Every time I go that way now I see that stain and think of those people and that splintered ball of human kindness, and of Billy. And wonder if, this time, he made it all the way to the Cemetery.

Angel in the playground

Laura K. Watson
[an extract]

NIGHT TIME. AN EMPTY PLAYGROUND.

Chloe (age14/15) has turned up with her 'friends' Manda & Nick
who, having humiliated her in front of Heather (age 10/11) & Josh,
have left her to go off clubbing. Heather and Josh are playing cards.
Chloe is off to the side, swinging the swing violently with her
hands. Heather watches her.

> HEATHER
> Are you sure you don't want to play?

Chloe carries on swinging the swing.

> CHLOE
> They won't talk to me again now.

HEATHER
Why do you care?

CHLOE
They're my friends.

HEATHER
They didn't seem that friendly to me.

Josh lays his cards down.

JOSH
Hey, you won!

HEATHER
(cheers)

A flicker of light rushes past Chloe, she ignores it.

HEATHER
Chloe, look!

The light has gone now.

CHLOE
What?

HEATHER
It's too late. You've missed it.

CHLOE
(to JOSH)
What's she on about?

JOSH
She keeps thinking she can see something.

HEATHER
You said you could see it too, you told that
Manda...

JOSH
I only said that to shut her up.

Chloe laughs. Heather throws her cards down.

HEATHER
Well, if it wasn't true, then why would so
many people be saying...

JOSH
But who have you actually heard say
anything for definite?

CHLOE
It's like that game where someone says
something to one person and they tell
someone else, only they change it a little and

then before you know it, it's completely
different from how it started.

JOSH
Chinese Whispers.

Heather looks down and starts turning the cards over and over as
though looking for something.

JOSH
And why would there suddenly be something
here now, as opposed to last year or the year
before, what's so special about now?

HEATHER
It's as good a time as any.

Josh goes to take the cards. Heather snatches them back.

CHLOE
I'm going.

She doesn't move. Heather continues turning over the cards.

HEATHER
Anyway, I know what it is.

CHLOE
Don't start.

HEATHER
I'm sure of it.

CHLOE
Heather!

HEATHER
I knew she'd come back... she wouldn't just
leave us forever, would she?

JOSH
Who are you talking about?

CHLOE
Nobody.

HEATHER
I mean, she must want to see us, her special
girls.

Chloe kicks the edge of the slide violently. Heather is almost in a
trance now.

JOSH
What is it?

Pause.

HEATHER
She was lying in her bed... the last time I saw
her... she had this white dress on, it was so pretty.

CHLOE
It was a hospital gown.

HEATHER
She was so pretty.

CHLOE
She'd lost most of her hair.

HEATHER
And there were white sheets on the bed and
this white background.

CHLOE
And tubes and machines and...

HEATHER
And it was like she was already there, like she
already was... an angel.

Pause.

JOSH
You're talking about your mum, aren't you?

Heather nods.

> CHLOE
> She was just a kid, she can't even remember.

> HEATHER
> *(leans in and whispers to JOSH)*
> She hates it when I tell that story, it's cos she
> gets a bit upset.

> CHLOE
> I hate it because it isn't true!... She was ill.
> She was in pain. She was ugly. And she left
> us... And she's not coming back... The thing
> with you Heather is that you think if you say
> something enough it'll come true, well it
> doesn't work like that.

Heather throws the cards everywhere before running off. Chloe and
Josh stare at each other. Slowly Josh picks up the scattered cards
and lays them out for another game. Chloe joins him.

> JOSH
> Are you OK?

> CHLOE
> Are you dealing or what?

The lights dim. Heather appears at the front of the stage. She stands alone. The flickering light appears again, circling Heather as though teasing her. To begin with Heather bats it away with her hands, as though wanting to get rid of it, then gradually starts chasing it again. She follows it off the stage.

Fade.

The lights come up. Silence. Chloe and Josh are playing cards.

> CHLOE
> Why are you here?

> JOSH
> I'm meant to be meeting someone.

> CHLOE
> Looks like they don't want to meet you.

They carry on playing cards, oblivious to the fact that Billy has finally arrived. He stands on the edge of the stage, watching. He won't enter the playground.

> JOSH
> Your turn.

As he says this, Josh looks up, dropping his hand of cards as he spots Billy. Billy edges away. Chloe looks up and starts laughing, somewhat nervously. Billy shrinks back even more. Josh gets up.

> JOSH
> I'd almost given up on you.

> BILLY
> What do you take me for – chicken?

Chloe's laughing gets more out of control.

> JOSH
> Why is she laughing at you?

> BILLY
> She's lost it – in the head – ever since her
> mum died... she's been nuttier than a snickers
> bar...

Chloe stops laughing. She gets up and approaches Billy, as though about to hit him. She stops herself at the last minute.

> CHLOE
> And you'd know all about that wouldn't you?

Billy and Chloe stare at each other. Billy turns to face Josh. He sets his feet apart and swings his arms.

BILLY
You ready then?

Pause.

JOSH
Aren't you coming in?

Pause.

BILLY
What's wrong with here?

JOSH
There isn't enough room really is there? ...I
like to spread myself out when I'm fighting.

BILLY
You? The only fighting you know how to do
is lying on the floor, crying!

CHLOE
Well, if its going to be that easy Billy, why
don't you cut him some slack and do as he
says. There's plenty of room in here.

Billy hesitates, takes a deep breath and steps in. The second he
steps inside the playground, he starts shaking. Josh is busy

bracing himself to fight, moving about as though he's in a boxing ring. Billy isn't paying attention. Josh takes a pop at him. Billy jumps and falls down.

At this moment Heather comes back, shocked to see Billy there. Billy pulls himself up again and flies towards Josh. They start fighting and chasing each other round. Chloe and Heather watch from the sidelines, Heather tries to move closer to Chloe, but she isn't having any of it.

Josh weaves in and out of the swings etc. Finally Billy catches hold of him and gets him down, leaning across the see-saw. Then he stops. He can't go on. Josh looks up at him, relief and suspicion mingled on his face.

Billy starts to sob. He drops his hand, lets go of Josh and sinks to the floor, sobbing uncontrollably.

Heather and Chloe exchange glances. Josh looks at them questioningly. Josh edges away from the crying Billy, though still sitting on the see-saw. Eventually Heather takes a step towards him, Chloe tries to pull her back, but Heather ignores her.

Slowly, very slowly, Heather leans down to touch Billy, unsure at first if he's going to shake her off or not. He doesn't. She holds him and strokes his hair. The crying subsides but Billy still doesn't raise his head.

HEATHER
You didn't need to come.

BILLY
I did... He said...

HEATHER
Josh wouldn't have minded.

Josh shakes his head, obviously confused.

JOSH
We could have gone somewhere else.

Pause.

BILLY
I thought I should... you know...

HEATHER
I know, but maybe it wasn't the time?

BILLY
No, that's just it. It is the time. I had to come,
you see I heard there was something here and
I... I thought.

HEATHER
You thought it might be Adam.

At the sound of Adam's name, Billy jerks his head up. Chloe gasps.

> CHLOE
> You're not supposed to talk about it.

> JOSH
> I don't understand.

Billy shakes his head.

> BILLY
> It's OK...

> HEATHER
> Of course it is... Everyone knows it was an
> accident.

Pause. Billy stares at her.

> JOSH
> Who's Adam?

Silence.

Chloe approaches the see-saw and sits on the floor beside Billy.

> CHLOE
> I remember the first time I saw you two. It
> was sports day. You were tiny, it must have

been in your first year... You were doing the sack race. Adam was in front, he had this bright red T-shirt on... you were a bit behind, determined to catch up with him... I remember, you hurled yourself forwards and grabbed his sack from behind... he fell straight down... he was so surprised, and I think you were too...

BILLY
He was angry at first.

CHLOE
But then he just started laughing and pulled you down with him.

BILLY
And we decided it would be more fun to race like that.

CHLOE
So you wriggled along like worms, giggling your heads off.

BILLY
We got disqualified in the end.

Pause.

CHLOE
I always used to look out for you after that,
watch you round school.

BILLY
Did you?

CHLOE
Yeah... You used to swap lunches too.

BILLY
His Mum always gave him peanut butter, he
hated it.

CHLOE
You used to give him your crisps...I just
thought it was great, the way you were
always laughing and always together...

Silence.

HEATHER
It's almost like he's here now.

She looks around, Josh follows her gaze. Billy shudders.

BILLY
That day... when it happened...

He stops and looks at Heather. She nods. He carries on.

> BILLY
> We were playing dares, you know, he'd dare
> me to do a roly-poly down the slide, I'd dare
> him to jump from one end of the see-saw to
> the next... It was getting dark...

> HEATHER
> It was a Sunday.

> CHLOE
> Everyone else had gone home for their tea.

> BILLY
> Adam had his Gran staying... he didn't want
> to go home, not yet. So we stayed...

> HEATHER
> The only ones left.

> BILLY
> And the dares got bigger... and better... but...

> CHLOE
> You don't have to do this.

Billy nods towards the swing. Josh edges back slightly, still unsure of what is going on. Billy takes a deep breath.

> BILLY
> We took it in turns, to push each other. If you
> go fast enough, and high enough, it's like all
> the colours of the sky and the playground and
> just everything are... It's like they're... dancing
> and you're dancing with them and you can
> see right past the colours, to the secret magic
> that's there inside.

Pause. Josh rocks the see-saw ever so slightly. Billy jumps. Josh stops.

> BILLY
> It was my turn to push Adam... I had these
> new trainers, bouncy, made me feel like a
> super-hero... and I just kept running and
> pushing and running and...

Heather takes his hand.

> BILLY
> Adam was laughing, I know he was... but... he
> was getting higher and higher, we were both
> going so fast... my trainers, the swing... my
> ears were buzzing... and then I sort of looked
> up and Adam had turned his head to look
> back at me, catch my attention, I don't know

and in between the colours and the pushing,
Adam's face loomed up and his eyes were really
big and even though there were all these
colours, his face looked really white... and
then I listened again, and he wasn't laughing...
he was screaming, telling me to stop, he felt
sick... but it was like I'd got caught up in the
pushing, my arms felt so strong and it was
like I was being lifted off the ground too...
flying... like I was the swing and I had these
new trainers and... and that's when I felt it.

JOSH
What? Felt what?

BILLY
All of a sudden, I was lighter... me... the swing...
and I looked up and... and he'd jumped or
fallen or... and he was on the ground... and
then I let go... and I was beside him...

He looks at Chloe.

BILLY
We were together, back together, like always,
only... he'd hit his head and...

Silence. Billy bows his head. Josh gets off the see-saw, walks, turns his back from the others .

> HEATHER
> I've seen something... here...

Billy looks up.

> CHLOE
> Ignore her, she's making it up.

> BILLY
> What is it? What have you seen?

> JOSH
> It's a light, a flickering light.

Heather looks at him in surprise. He still has his back to them.

> JOSH
> It's like it's teasing you. The minute you think
> you've got it, it's gone.

> BILLY
> But what is it?

> CHLOE
> It's nothing.

HEATHER
I think it's whatever you want it to be.

Chloe raises her eyebrows.

BILLY
I've got this big picture in my head, of Adam,
just after he... And behind it there's all these
other little pictures of him, working in class,
eating his lunch, swimming, running, laughing...
and it's like the little pictures are trying to
get through, to the front of my head, the
front of my memory, only the big picture's too
big and it's taking up all the space...

CHLOE
It was an accident Billy. You were friends.
Best friends.

Josh turns back to face Billy and the others.

JOSH
I get it now.

Billy looks at him.

BILLY
You started talking to me, just after you moved in.

JOSH
I thought you looked lonely.

BILLY
You wouldn't leave me alone.

JOSH
It was like you were waiting for someone.

BILLY
Told me about your pet dog...

JOSH
Only they never showed up.

BILLY
You wouldn't shut up... I didn't want to like you... I didn't want you to...

JOSH
You didn't want me to be your friend.

Billy shakes his head.
The lights fade. In the darkness the light can be seen flickering back and forth across the stage.

You
go down between the
dark and foxy walls of the
corridor past the two bars at the
front, past the toilets and the
cigarette machine, to the back bar
and you know why you're there
again, with Hachimi tonight
but sometimes without
him.

Snookered

Rosie Ford

You're in your usual pumps and the grey
sweater that's too tight and too hot, and
jeans, and they all know you, with your pale
face and long hair. And the promising lights
are up all over the place, behind the bar, in
the corner lamps, but more promising than
any is the hooded light over the green baize of
the snooker table. The drinks are always the
same, the cider and the beer, so exactly cold, yours and
his. It's not only him you've come for, though he's part of you,
an attachment. You've come for the loucheness in tall Harry's
sky-blue eyes, for the big belly on teasing Walter who always
says hello, for toothless Brian who always says he wishes you
wore skirts. At the far end of the room, Gareth is leaning out
of the window on this close night, double-sided Gareth, sweet
breath on your cheek one minute, setting his mother's house
on fire the next.

You'd like to be always there chalking up your initials
on the blackboard, unzipping your plastic cue case taking out
the two varnished parts and screwing them together, slowly
as if putting off the pleasure, as if there were some problem
with the thread, as if you were calm and expecting nothing.

Hachimi's there with you, and so is Wendy, with eyes
like oval buttonholes and skin you'd die for, and frizzy-haired
Gill in the pink mini-skirt wanting Brian to kiss her teethful
mouth. They like being women. And on the other side is Jill

who looks like Joan Baez, as tall as Zambian Theo, her lover, and Hachimi is tender, lighting your roll-up with his Zippo. There's talk of rights and the Right, how to sleep in the heat and what needs changing outside these walls. From the adjoining room, you can hear the plaintive music - Oh Daddy, if I could make you see. If there's been a fool around, it's got to be me.

But the music isn't it; that huge, green and heavy-legged island in the middle of the room is it. You look at it because you have to. You face it, all the time, all of you sitting on those cool grey plastic covered benches with your backs to the walls. You're watching the film of a game, the story of the white cue ball, what can be done with it if you really know how. Your cue's the prompter, the conductor's baton, your aim to play the silly pizzicata of the dizzy, coloured balls and then the ultimate black ball that's genderless.

Why are you right and I'm so wrong? I'm so weak and you're so strong, the singer wonders, as well she might, in the other room where old men sit where they've always sat and young men on a loud stag night are wearing suspenders.

Outside it may be raining in the neon-lit night. In winter there may be the thick frost that ices the pavements by opening time. Down the road, the corner grocer may be held up at gunpoint behind his manual till but you're here at the green felt's edge with a cocktail of plain salted crisps and dry roasted nuts, a large black ashtray and the cold pint half gone now.

Then it's your turn. Someone's just potted the black ball and he's the star for the next few minutes but now it's you and Hachimi playing doubles, looking for that ephemeral solution. (Is that what he's after too?) You're playing against Walter with the belly and Vijay, all in black – shirt, hair and trousers. You're chalking your cue tip to be sure there's no slipping, no skidding, no missing the point, and so are they. The chalk's a little cube of blue, a miniature crater. It's shared, and then it's down to business. We're all half serious but Vijay's the best.

You strip off your sweater like a man, pulling it over your head from behind and your pink T-shirt rides up your bare white back and they whistle, the boys, but all you want, now you're 36, is the black ball of being only another player.

Who's going to break? You toss a coin and win and give the break to Walter and you're glad it's not yours. There's no vantage-ground when the reds explode like that, shifting the pink only a little and leaving the black hovering over the bottom pocket. You wish that black was yours and you'd score 8 in all to make your mark at the beginning. You know it won't be. Vijay's practised eye will take it easily after you've had your turn and blown it. Your cue guesses the exact spot on the surface of the cue ball that will tuck that red ball into the middle pocket at an angle of 45 degrees. You eye it, feel it, then you shoot hoping it will pull back for the black as well, but it hits the cushion 2 centimetres from the pocket's lip, so the red's not yours and neither is the black.

They are Vijay's in 90 seconds flat.

Everything you do is just all right. And I can't get away from you, baby, if I try, she sings conclusively. The young men in the other room are waiting for the strip-a-gram.

And so on. It's the same as usual standing at the end of the beer-breathing table, holding your cue with both hands in front of you as if you were Tensing viewing Everest watching the way men care and not care whether they win or lose and neither do you and that's the truth. But you want that black ball badly in the middle of the game, or better still at the end when the recognition lasts longer.

Somewhere else Russia may be invading Afghanistan, Thatcher may be in drag, waiting in the wings with the cue ball in her hand, but this snooker room is filling up with smoke. Your roll-up rests in the ashtray between turns, as does Hachimi's and Walter's and Vijay's. Gareth complains about the length of the game but he's not been watching how close it is on the baize. Walter puts more money in the light meter. You look at the scoreboard on the wall by the door; it's 40 to them on the top, 29 to you and him on the bottom. It's anyone's game with only one red left on the table. Hachimi takes the red and the yellow, that's 32. Walter fouls on the cue ball, that's 36 to the two of you. Then it's your turn. The green is over the pocket and you slam it in, that's 39.

But the brown comes next and it's almost on the cushion at the other end of the table and you're supposed to play it safe and you don't know how to do that. It's an intuitive game you play, not like the rest but they don't know that. You lean over the table, eye up the brown ball quickly and go hard. Unexpectedly it re-doubles against the cushion at a slight angle and rolls very quickly the full length of the table and into a bottom pocket. You gasp, they thump their cues on the carpeted floor enthusiatically and then you try for the blue, with the same bravado. It's about 80 centimetres from the other top pocket. And it's yours again! You're not better than them, you're the same when your wind's in the right direction. The thumping of cues and the whooping voices make you smile. They're all there with you including Gareth now but you fail on the pink which means, of course, there'll be no black for you tonight. There's moisture on your forehead near the hairline. With the tip of your cue you slide the brass finger on the bottom row of the scoreboard to 48. It's 43 - 48 and it's Vijay's turn. He cleans up as he often does. You watch the black ball go down and there's talk of his mis-spent youth and you all shake hands. Hachimi tries to kiss you because he thinks he knows what you wanted to do, but you're putting your sweater on and unscrewing your cue.

When you go home, you lean the cue in the corner of the hall below the coats, against the feather duster and the hockey sticks and run upstairs to say goodnight to your daughters. The youngest one's bedroom is nearly dark. In the orange light from the street you can see her eyes are closed but fluttering. You can't hear her sleeping-breath. On the desk by the bed and on the floor her school books are scattered. The other daughter's light is on. She's sitting at her desk paraphrasing, she tells you, a soliloquoy of Lady Macbeth. She doesn't look up.

Shouldn't you have stayed at home and helped us with our homework? they ask, twenty years later, when they are women who've never played snooker.

Would have been quicker

to fly.

[bus driver to two girls wearing wireframe fairy wings]

Notes on contributors

DON BARNARD qualified in Arabic, then switched to computers in 1963. His move to performance poetry in 1997 confirmed he could still spot a trend and ride it without qualifications or talent. His MA studies at Hallam are something else.

MARY BONNER gained a wonderful circle of friends from Sheffield Hallam - as well as the MA in Writing in 2001. She recently left her second part-time job as a primary school teaching assistant to spend more time writing. This is her second published story.

BRYONY DORAN was born in a Youth Hostel on Dartmoor and brought up in Cornwall. She studied Fashion at Manchester University and, since her son was born, has run her own clothing business. Bryony moved to Sheffield in 1990 where she again took up writing. She is currently writing a novel.

MICHEL FABER was born in Holland in 1960, grew up in Australia and now lives in the Scottish highlands. A collection of his award-winning short stories was followed by the novel Under The Skin, which was sold to 21 countries and shortlisted for the Whitbread Prize. His fifth and latest book is The Crimson Petal And The White.

ROSIE FORD is a writer of poetry and fiction who lives in Derbyshire. She has published in several magazines and is the founder of The Kitley Trust which promotes creative writing especially in schools.

JANICE GALLOWAY is the author of five critically celebrated works of fiction. Her first novel, The Trick is to keep Breathing, now widely regarded as a Scottish contemporary classic, was published in 1990, shortlisted for the Whitbread First Novel, Scottish First Book and Aer Lingus Awards, and won the MIND/Allan Lane Book of the Year. Her second book, Blood, shortlisted for the Guardian Fiction Prize, People's Prize and Satire Award, was a New York Times Notable Book of the Year. Her second novel, Foreign Parts, won the McVitie's Prize in 1994. Janice's new novel, Clara, based in the life of pianist Clara Wieck Schumann, was published by Cape in June 2002.

NIYATI KENI is a London based writer. Current projects – a novel, sci-fi short stories and scripts for theatre. Vital stats – short, sane, female. The Curtain will be appearing in the London fringe later this year.

PETER DANIELS LUCZINSKI has twice been a winner of the Poetry Business Competition, most recently with the pamphlet Through the Bushes (Smith/Doorstop, 2000). He has edited anthologies for the Oscars Press, and worked for Poetry London from 1994 to 2001. He is on the MA Writing course at Sheffield Hallam.

E.A. MARKHAM was born on the West Indian island of Montserrat in 1939. He grew up in London in the 1950s and read English and Philosophy at university. He has been involved in editing Ambit, Artrage and Writing Ulster magazines, and Sheffield Thursday. He has published six collections of poetry and two of short stories. His publications include Misapprehensions (poetry, Anvil 1995), The Penguin Book of Caribbean Short Stories (1996), A Papua New Guinea Sojourn: More Pleasures of Exile (travel, Carcanet 1998), Marking Time (a 'campus' novel, Peepal Tree Press, 1999) and A Rough Climate (poetry and prose, Anvil, 2002). In 1997 Markham was awarded a Certificate of Honour by the Government of Montserrat.

L.V. O'REILLY was born in Dublin and has taught in both Ireland and England. She currently lectures in English and Creative Writing in Sheffield and Rotheram.

TRACEY O'ROURKE lives in Sheffield and teaches creative writing at Sheffield Hallam University. She is co-editor of Proof.

SHELLEY ROCHE is a poet on the Sheffield Hallam Writing MA.

SUSAN SHAW'S writing is influenced by a background in visual arts. She has received a Year Of The Artist award and, currently, a research and development award (literature) from Yorkshire Arts. She is now working on a collection of short stories that range from 200 to 2,500 words in length.

ALI SMITH was born in Inverness in 1962 and lives in Cambridge. Her first collection of stories Free Love won the Saltire First Book Award and a Scottish Arts Council Award in 1995. Her first novel, Like, was published in 1997 and her second collection of stories, Other Stories and Other Stories, in 1999. Her latest novel, Hotel World, was published in 2001 and shortlisted for the Booker and the Orange Prize for Fiction.

JASON STARMER spent his childhood in South Africa and later moved to London. He lives in Soho and is finishing his first novel whilst working as a waiter in the West End.

LAURA K. WATSON has just finished the teaching part of the MA Writing, specialising in script, and was lucky enough to be supported by an AHRB Post-graduate Award. She had her first play, Nightcap, broadcast in March on Radio 4. Laura is currently living in London and working as a Script Editor on EastEnders.

CAROLYN WAUDBY is a journalist and poet who lives in Sheffield and lectures in journalism at the universities of Sheffield and Leeds. Her poem on wind turbines was turned into a short film 'Not Born of the Earth' for millennium celebrations in Barnsley. She has just published 'Bouquet', a booklet of poems based on contemporary art works, with the aid of a Yorkshire Arts grant.

TONY WILLIAMS lives and works in Sheffield and is a student on the MA Creative Writing course at Sheffield Hallam University. 'Rhetoric', a pamphlet of poems, was published by Mews Press in 2000.

www.mattermagazine.co.uk
contact: mattermagazine@yahoo.co.uk

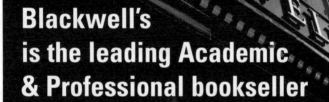

If you write, read

Mslexia

Plugged-in and informative *Mslexia* is at the cutting edge of women's writing today. Packed with news, reviews, features, advice and practical information on how and where to get your work published. *Mslexia* is the essential read for women who write, who want to write, who teach creative writing, who have an interest in women's literature, or who just want to write for fun.

For a NO-RISK TRIAL subscription call 0191 261 6656 or write to Mslexia (Mk), PO Box 656, Freepost NEA5566, Newcastle upon Tyne, NE99 2RP

mktrial@mslexia.demon.co.uk

Supported by the National Lottery through the Arts Council of England and Northern Arts